THE WISDOM LUNCH WARRIOR

PRAISE FOR
THE WISDOM LUNCH WARRIOR

*"It's a 150 page adventure. I didn't just read the **Wisdom Lunch Warrior** I devoured it and you will too...life changing."*

Mark Schlereth
ESPN Analyst, 3-Time Superbowl Champion

*"We talk a great deal about the 'Whole Man' concept as a leader in the Teams and the **Wisdom Lunch Warrior** is a blue print in story form for how to be a complete leader."*

Gary Denham
Director of Instructor Training Navy Special Warfare Center
U.S. Navy SEAL (Retired)

*"If culture eats vision for lunch, the **Wisdom Lunch Warrior** will give you a vision for who you can and need to be as a leader of culture in today's world."*

Jeff Banister
Manager, Texas Rangers MLB

"Coach O has done it again!!! Leadership experts agree - your organization needs a mentoring program. But unlike the others, Rod shows you how. In The Wisdom Lunch, Rod demonstrates the power of deliberate and creative investment in future leaders, all in the midst of a powerful, feel-good story unlike the myriad books on the topic."

Jeffrey D. Sweetin
DEA Special Agent (Retired)
Director of Training Academy, Quantico
U.S. Drug Enforcement Administration

"Rod Olson's book is a practical "coaching manual" for any leader with a strong desire to make a radical and positive difference in their organization as well as their personal leadership walk! I have known Rod Olson for years and submit that his book, the "Wisdom Lunch" captures his desire for leaders to be transformed personally and professionally by turning selfish desires into selfless aspirations. It is a must read for all leaders who have a desire to succeed in their respective organizations."

James L. Capra
CEO/ Front Line Leadership Group
Author of Leadership at the Front Line

"The Wisdom Lunch is a great read! Rod expertly ties his principles into this parable story. Leaders in all facets of life will find that these principles will help them grow and mature. Even more importantly, these principles will help them to transform their whole organization.

Doug Dawson
Owner, Colorado Pediatric Home Care

Wow! Coach O has done it again. Powerful leadership insights and attitudes are clearly and concisely communicated in the sequel ...... The Wisdom Lunch. Having personally experienced both sides of a Wisdom Lunch I can tell you it is an impactful and transforming process for all parties involved.

John Seiple
President, Huntington Industrial Partners

"You need to read this book. Every person has a story and Rod Olson shares in story format what he has learned from others. In Rod's second book he teaches the richness and importance of accountability and the tools to being more effective and a difference maker in any organization".

Bob Parry, Director A.C.E.
Achieving Community Excellence, City of Greeley

THE WISDOM LUNCH WARRIOR

"5 Marks of a Mature Leader"

ROD OLSON

THE LEGACY BUILDER

Published by Rod Olson Consulting

Printed and Distributed by Cross Training Publishing

15418 Weir Street #177

Omaha, NE 68137 U.S.A.

Rod Olson

Rod@coachesofexcellence.com

720-479-8100

Paperback ISBN 978-1-938254-46-8

© 2015 Rod Olson

Cover Design: Fuller Creative Inc.

Printed in the United States of America

First Edition 2015

CONTENTS

FOREWORD

It has been said that when the pupil is ready the master will appear, well the Master has appeared and you can learn from him in *The Wisdom Lunch Warrior*. We live in a world that is starving for mature authentic leaders and as a businessman myself, I am always in search of ways to sharpen my leadership skills. As a former professional athlete and father, I see how many organizations are in dire need of finding and developing world class coaches. *The Wisdom Lunch Warrior* solves the problem of underdeveloped leadership.

The Wisdom Lunch Warrior takes you on a simple yet gripping journey toward self discovery and growth through the eyes of a young man that needs it desperately. I didn't so much read this book as much as I devoured it.

In my talks with Rod Olson, we have discussed many ideas on coaching and leadership, but in *The Wisdom Lunch Warrior* Rod does a masterful job of drawing upon his work with top leaders from multiple industries, and by writing in his compelling leadership fable format, he makes you want to seek out and arrange "wisdom lunches" with mentors for your own personal journey. This book is a must read for anyone who has a desire to grow leaders in today's world or has a hunger to be the best they can be personally, professionally and spiritually.

Maturity isn't about changing who you are, it's about gaining wisdom and growing as a leader. If you are ready to be challenged and grow, *The Wisdom Lunch Warrior* is for you. *Enjoy!*

Mark Schlereth
ESPN Analyst, 3-Time Superbowl Champion

*To the late Frosty Westering,
the best coach that you may have never
heard of, a friend, mentor and true Legacy Builder.*

CHAPTER ONE

Life Takes a Turn

Lance Marshall looked up from his laptop, peering over his reading glasses at his wife, Amanda. After a light dinner, the two of them had fallen into their regular evening routine, stretching out on the sectional, Amanda on one end and Lance on the other, their legs leaning against each other in the middle. This was their "together time," and, as usual, Lance had been journaling and planning out the next day while Amanda read on her tablet.

But Lance had noticed that his distracted wife had not touched the screen for almost fifteen minutes, her stare at some distant point.

Lance nudged her affectionately with his foot. "Still thinking about the baby shower?"

Her gentle smile warmed his heart, as it had since he'd first seen her in home room when they were both juniors in high school. She shook her head. "No, although we all had a really good time."

"Connie was pleased? You went to a lot of trouble for our darling daughter."

Amanda smiled. "Not that much trouble. But she was ecstatic.

And they kept passing around the ultrasound pictures we saw last week." She looked out the back door, staring into the dark of their expansive backyard.

"So what's up?"

She shook her head. "You know. I want to tell her. And I don't."

Lance closed his laptop and set it aside. "We agreed we wouldn't tell anyone but Keli before the baby was born. I don't want the children stressed, but I knew he could handle it."

"I know. He's your best friend." She closed her tablet's case, set it aside and scooted over to snuggle in next to him. "It's just hard." Amanda slid her hand into his, clutching it tightly. "The baby won't be here for another three months. And you'll be starting chemotherapy in a few days. It'll be even harder to keep quiet then."

Lance pulled his hand free and wrapped his arms around her. "But we will. They just don't need the stress right now. Robert needs to focus on his dissertation, and Connie and David have enough to worry about, with his new position as well as the baby. And Tony. . ." His words drifted off, thinking about the severity of Tony's disabilities. Would he even understand the nature of the illness? Still, he should be told. "After the birth, we'll have a family meeting. OK?"

She nodded, then peered up at him. "So you have decided on what you'll do with the company? David?"

He nodded. "I'm going to bring David up as my successor." Lance waited, watching Amanda closely. After more than thirty-five years, he knew his wife would react honestly. He depended on it.

She didn't disappoint. Amanda drew away and stared at him. "Are you sure? I know you love our son-in-law, but do you think he's ready? He's only twenty-nine! He's only led one small team, and they were already go-getters when he took charge. Will your board go for this?"

Lance let out a long breath, weary. Fatigue came sooner than it used to, and seemed more encompassing, part and parcel of developing cancer. "I wondered about that. I've been talking with Keli about him." He shifted a bit. "Do you remember how you set me up with Coach Moore for those mentoring sessions?"

She nodded. "It's been ten years, but you don't forget something like that. It changed your life. Our lives. Those lessons about being a Legacy Builder completely changed how you saw yourself, your company, and our marriage. Are you thinking about doing something similar with David?"

"Keli and I have been discussing it. I think it's the only way the board will accept him—and I believe it's best way to get him ready for it. He's got the right skill sets, enough ambition and drive. He just needs more maturity as a leader. I think this will get him there. Plus, you know there's a unexpected surprise for him in the mix."

"I doubt he'll be ready for that. I don't know anyone who could be."

"But it'll push him. Challenge him. Right now, he needs that."

"You're going to spring this on him tomorrow?"
"Right after the board meeting."
Amanda stood and reached for his hand. "Then you need some rest. And maybe some extra inspiration."

Lance laughed and got up, pulling her into his arms. "You always were my best encourager. I love you."

CHAPTER TWO

Ambitious Dreams

David Jeffress tried desperately not to fidget. Or pace. Both habits his father-in-law had cautioned him to fight, and he knew Lance's assistant was watching him, even though she appeared not to. Terry's desk sat front and center in the plush executive office suite, square between the boardroom and Lance's office, and directly in front of a smaller conference room and the office of the corporate communications VP. David had grasped early in his career that while Lance headed the company, Terry was its heart. She knew as much about the running of this company as Lance did.

A good reason to keep her when I take over. David's leg bounced, his body trying to keep up with his racing thoughts, his anxiety to get this part over with. He stood and turned to stare at a piece of art on the wall, one he'd already seen hundreds of times.

President. I'll be president of a nationally acclaimed company. Well, second-in-line for now. But I'm only twenty-nine. He grinned. It had not been his planned path when he met Connie Marshall at a college mixer five years ago. She'd been a freshman on the volleyball team; he'd been in his last year as the football team's quarterback. They'd been a perfect match from the beginning, definitely the best thing that had ever happened to David. They'd waited a couple of years to get married, and David had wanted to go into sports psychology, like Connie's brother, Robert. Instead, Lance had offered him a place here, if David would wait until Connie finished school before heading to grad school.

David still remembered his first week at the company. He had taken Lance's offer, but had chafed at the idea. Working for his father-in-law. How cliché. Boring. David had offended everyone he worked with for almost a month, until Lance had subtly suggested that the worth of an employee was only partially based on the work he did. And he had done so without insulting David. It had been the first time David realized that Lance was going to be far more than his father-in-law.

Grad school never happened. David loved the work, and in the first two years, he'd been promoted twice by his own supervisors—not by Lance. The money was great, of course, but there were other perks. A terrific benefits package. Travel. A type of fame from the presentations he made at conferences. People ask him for advice.

And now Lance stood in front of the board, recommending they make David second-in-command of the entire company.

What is taking them so long? This should be a cinched deal! I'm good. I can do this!

Well, it was also a giant leap up the corporate ladder. But surely they could see he'd proved himself. He knew some people would be jealous, resentful, thinking that he got the job because of being married to Connie, but he could deal with that. He'd have the power to deal with anyone who came at him.

And the money! David's grin broadened, and he shifted his weight from one foot to the other, his fantasies expanding rapidly.

A Mercedes. Maybe two. Connie would need one for her and the baby. The big ones, maybe a matched set . . . no, a red one for her. A new house, one in a planned community, with a golf course attached. He'd love to do business while golfing, maybe have lunch with Connie before one of her tennis lessons. . . .

"Mr. Jeffress?"

David jerked around. "Yes?"

Terry left her desk and went to the boardroom door, opening it. "They'll see you now."

CHAPTER THREE

The Succession Plan

David entered the room, and Lance recognized the tension in his son-in-law's steps, the shallow breaths, the light sheen of sweat on his face. Of course, he'd be anxious.

Lance hadn't been fully free of nerves himself that morning, and it had taken more than an hour to convince his reluctant board that David was right for the job, and that the plan of "Wisdom Lunches" would be the right path, the perfect next step in David's maturing as a leader. Even with Keli by his side as he had been for the last few years, two votes had been required before they were all convinced to give David a chance.

Now, if David would only agree to this . . .

Lance glanced at up at Keli as the big man moved to take his seat next to him. At six-foot-eight and almost two hundred and seventy five pounds, Keli had been a huge presence in Lance's life for the past decade, helping hold him accountable and to stay consistent with the lessons Lance had learned ten years ago. Although he was two years younger, Keli had been one of Lance's mentors. His reminders that Lance's own life and business had been "out of control" before he had undergone a similar type of mentoring, finally swayed the last two board members. Lance has worked hard to pass on the same principles

Now it was time to take David to the next step.

of focus, balance, and positive relationships to David, and had watched most of them take hold in the younger man.

Now it was time to take David to the next step.

Lance motioned for David to take the remaining seat at the table. As David settled, Lance took a deep breath and plunged in. "David, as you realize, this session of the board was called to determine my successor, someone with the appropriate skills and leadership potential to lead the company after I step down."

David nodded, and Lance continued. "While we have all agreed that you have the necessary skills, there has been a lack of confidence that you have the comparable maturity and ability to lead the wide variety of teams that make up our biggest asset, our employees."

Lance watched closely as David stiffened, his face growing red. Too much anger, too soon. As his son-in-law inhaled, preparing to speak, Lance held up one hand. "Wait. Allow me to continue." Nearby, two of the board members shifted uncomfortably in their chairs. This was what they had been worried about. David's youth.

The quick temper.

Lance went on. "What we've agreed to is a series of meetings with you and each of the board members. Wisdom Lunches, if you will. They will share with you one quality that they have learned over the years is essential in a mature leader." He gestured to his right. "Keli and I will oversee these. After each meeting, you'll debrief with us, including a description of how you plan to adopt each quality and apply it to your everyday life, as well as your work.

"If you agree to these, then when the meetings are complete, we'll convene another board meeting and if everyone agrees with your growth and plans for development, you'll be formally voted in as my successor. What do you say?"

David remained silent for a few moments, and Lance could see the muscles in David's jaw tighten as he looked around the room at each board member. Lance realized this definitely was not what his son-in-law had expected, and he respected the hesitation.

"I realize," Lance continued, "this isn't a direction you were expecting, but we feel it's the right one, to help you grow into what could be a grounded and successful tenure here. You know Keli, of course. The other members you'll be meeting with will be John Holliday, Jr., owner and director of the Holliday Speedway."

John, Jr., a fit-looking man in his early seventies, sat at Keli's right. He nodded at David, a thick shock of white hair falling down over his forehead. Lance gestured to the African-American woman sitting on his left. "You may recognize Marla Patterson from the sports pages. She's the former NCAA division one head women's basketball coach, and she's won two national titles and has now transitioned to being the first female Athletic Director at the University in town here. She'll meet with you after John Jr."

"I look forward to it, David," Marla said.

"To Marla's left is Gary Fullmer, who is Commander of the Navy SEALs special warfare center, and to John Jr.'s right is Denny Storm, who led one of the most successful chains of hotels. He may be retired, but he still mentors young entrepreneurs and is an active volunteer in a number of ministries. Keli will be your last meeting, as well as being in the debriefing sessions with me. Keli will be on the board for some time to come, and I want you to be able to come to him anytime."

During this last speech, Lance had watched some of the tension ease away from David, as his face softened and his shoulders drop. Resignation. He's realized this has to happen. Lance nodded at David, encouraging him to speak.

David swallowed hard. "When will these meetings start? I'll need to get them on my calendar."

Keli spoke, "We'll give Terry a number of possible dates, then she'll set them up with you." A move geared to get David and

Terry more familiar with each other.

He and Lance stood, prompting David to stand as well. "I'll talk with you tomorrow if you have any questions."

His son-in-law nodded, then turned and left.

Keli looked at Lance. "He's furious. Now I know why you held this meeting at the end of the day. He's going to have to cool off."

Lance smiled. "Yep. Remind you of someone?"

Keli laughed. "Let's just hope he gets wise as fast as you did."

* * *

David fumed, muttering under his breath as he left the executive suite. Back in his cubicle, he dropped into his chair, glaring at the hard gray walls. "'Wisdom Lunches,' who is he kidding? Why not just tell me I have to interview with everyone on the board?" He slammed his briefcase and got up, yanking it off the desk. As he headed out of the cubicle, he kicked the trash can, watching it scatter balls of paper on the floor. "Whatever."

He strode out of the building, ignoring the main desk receptionist and the security guard, both of whom nodded at him. David tossed the case in the back seat then slide behind the wheel of his Jeep Wrangler. The rage he felt had begun to devolve into annoyance, and a general sense of failure settled over him. "What does he want from me!"

He backed the Wrangler out of the space, and thumbed his phone, calling his wife. When she answered, David felt an immediate sense of relief. Sweet Connie. Someone who understood. "What is your father thinking?"

Connie hesitated. "What are you talking about? How did it go? Didn't you get the job?"

"No!" He explained about the series of Wisdom Lunches, his words tumbling over each other. "I thought he liked me. Why would he prep me for this interview if the job wasn't going to happen?"

Connie sighed. "Did he explain that he went through something like this about ten years ago?"

"What are you talking about?"

"Daddy was . . . a loose cannon. We all hated him, even Mother. Well, 'hate' may be too strong. Despise. The company was doing OK, but he wasn't a good man anymore. Mother was super close to leaving him, although I don't think she's ever mentioned it to him."

The thought of losing Connie swept over David like a cold wave. "Seriously? She would leave him?"

"He's different now. You didn't know him then. He was angry. Selfish. Every bit of his self worth was wrapped up in the job. In a last-ditch effort, Mother convinced him to go see his high school coach. Coach Moore set Daddy up with a series of mentors, and they really changed his life. And ours."

"So he thinks I need to change my life? That's pretty arrogant!"

Connie sighed. "Maybe he just thinks you could benefit from people who've been-there and done-that."

David stopped at a red light. It couldn't hurt to talk to folks who've walked the same path before. What Connie said made sense, but . . .

> "It couldn't hurt to talk to folks who've walked the same path before."

28

"He could have warned me."

"Would you have accepted
the meetings if the job wasn't waiting at the end?"

He blinked twice as her words hit home. "I . . . I probably
wouldn't have found the time," he admitted.

"Taken the time," she responded, her voice soft.

The light turned green. "How is it you know me so well?"

"Because I love you. Comes with the territory." She paused.
"Come home, sweetheart. Dinner's about ready. You tell me about
your meeting, I'll tell you about Daddy, and we'll listen to the baby."
"Sounds like a plan." David ended the connection, feeling better.
Despite the left turn the meeting took, life was good, and his future
was looking better than ever.

CHAPTER FOUR

The Day the World Stopped

David crossed his arms, the chill he'd felt for the past two days intensifying. Funeral parlors are always so cold! He shuddered, cold and numb. He felt grateful to be a little numb, which was infinitely preferable to the grief that had wrecked him since Connie had gotten the call from her mother, and they had rushed to the hospital. He still had a hard time accepting that the man in the casket on the far end of the room would never speak to him again. Never clap him on the shoulder and tell him what a good job he'd done. How proud he was of David as his son-in-law.

How could he have been so sick and no one know? That board meeting had been just over a week earlier. He knew Lance had taken some time off . . . .

Keli stepped up beside him and handed David a pallbearer's boutonniere. "How you holding up?"

> ## "I feel as if the world has stopped."

David had kept his football physique, but even at six-one he had to look up at Keli. "Not well. You?"

Keli shook his head. "I feel as if the world has stopped. It'll take some time."

"Why didn't he tell us?"

"He didn't want to add to the stress of having a new baby. He never thought he'd die. Did they tell you . . . ?"

David let out a long breath. "Something about his body reacting badly to the chemo. The cancer was worse than they thought, and when pneumonia set in, they couldn't stop it. He went down so fast . . . ." His words trailed off, and David turned back to stare at the casket, inserting the boutonniere in his coat without looking. "I still can't believe it."

"Have you talked with anyone from work?"

"Not since I made the announcement about . . . you know we've shut down for a week?"

Keli nodded. "Best plan. And you'll need to address it when everyone returns. Talk to HR about setting up some counselors."

David stared at him. "Me?"

Keli's eyebrows arched. "Yes. There'll be some transition period, but all the VPs, and the board, knew you were his handpicked successor. Lance didn't expect to die, but he did expect to be too sick to mentor you. He . . . left some things for you. Videos you'll need to watch."

"I don't know if I can do this."

"He believed you could."

David stared out one of the parlor windows. "Did he ever tell you that I didn't know my real dad?"

"No, he didn't. He wouldn't share something private like that."

"When I met Connie, when I met Lance and Amanda, I understood for the first time what a real family, a loving family was like. Connie used to kid me that we now shared the same father." He paused. "She was joking, but she was right. I knew I could be a good dad to our kids because I could see how Lance was with his family."

Keli cleared his throat. "Lance wasn't always a great dad, but he was a warrior."

"Connie told me."

"Let's meet next week in the boardroom. Before the company comes back."

> "Lance wasn't always a great dad, but he was a warrior."

33

"Sure."

"Is someone bringing Tony?"

David paused. He hadn't thought about Lance and Amanda's second son much since Lance's death. He'd been too focused on Connie and his own grief. Severely handicapped, Tony had lived in a group home for the past five years, where they helped him interact with other individuals with disabilities as well as the community. "No. They've told him, but Amanda didn't think he could handle the service."

"Understandable. Will your mother be here?"

"Yes." David gave a bitter laugh. "She flew in so we could celebrate my promotion. Her flight leaves this afternoon."

Keli suddenly grabbed David's shoulders and turned the younger man toward him. He then straightened David's tie and the drooping boutonniere. "He will be proud of you. Always was. Still is."

David nodded, not trusting his voice any longer. Keli was right. His world had stopped. And it would never be the same again.

* * *

The next three hours passed in a daze. The remaining viewing time—when he tried to comfort Connie as best he could—gave way to a funeral filled with praise for a man gone far too soon. Speaker after speaker told about the impact Lance had made on their lives. The support and guidance he'd offered. Lance had not been an old man, but he'd already created a remarkable legacy.

David knew the chapel had been filled to capacity, but even more people turned out at the graveside service, crowding in around the family and extending out across the grounds and toward a peaceful lake in the center. His mother had arrived just before the service began and had stayed by his side at the grave. As the pastor read the last Bible verse, he asked if anyone else wanted to say a final word. David's chest tightened. He'd kept silent in the chapel, but now the urge to speak was like a hand shoving at his back. He swallowed the lump in his throat and gestured to the pastor. "I would."

He turned toward the crowd. "Earlier, I asked Keli if he knew that I never knew my real dad, that he'd died before I was born. Keli responded that Lance would never have shared something so private. Which speaks volumes about the man Lance was. But I don't need that to be private. I need everyone to know that the gap, the hole that my father left in my life had been filled by Lance Marshall. I didn't even realize that hole could be filled, didn't realize how much I needed a dad, until he stepped into it. He accepted me into his family. He welcomed me as Connie's husband but also as if I were his third son. He demonstrated, every day, what a real man is like, and if I'm half the father to my children that he was to me, then they'll grow up to be terrific people. I only hope I can live up to the legacy he left behind."

> "I only hope I can live up to the legacy he left behind."

David's voice broke and he stepped back, and Connie grabbed his arm, sobbing into his shoulder. His mother looked up at him, then away quickly.

The pastor said a final prayer, then everyone fell silent as the casket was lowered. At the back of the crowd, some folks began to wander back toward the cars. Near the grave, the funeral director began speaking softly to Amanda, Robert, and Connie. David stepped toward them, but felt a tug on his arm. He looked down at his mother.

Abigail Jeffress had turned fifty a month ago, but every year had carved creases across her face. Tears streaked through her makeup, etching the lines around her eyes and mouth even deeper. "David," she whispered. "I must talk to you."

He glanced back at the Marshall family. "Can this not wait?"

"No. I have a cab waiting. I didn't want you to leave them to take me to the airport, but I have to go. I need to tell you something. Now."

He fought the urge to snap at her. Connie needed him. But Abigail was his mother. He took her arm and led her over to a lush maple near the grave. They stood in the shade. "OK. Tell me."

Abigail clenched a ball of tissue in one fist as she pressed the other hand to her mouth. She trembled, shivering as if she were freezing despite the warm day.

He crossed his arms. "What is it? I need to get back to Connie."

She straightened her shoulders. "What you said. About your father. About him being dead."

"What about it?"

"I . . . I didn't—" Her voice broke, and she inhaled deeply, trying again. "I thought it was for the best. He wasn't going to be around because of his business. We weren't married."

A fire speared through David's gut. No. No . . . she couldn't mean . . . "What are you saying?"

"I told him that if he couldn't marry me . . . if we couldn't be a family, then he needed to never come back. Better that you thought him dead."

David staggered back, as pole-axed as if a linebacker had blind sided him. "He's alive?"

She nodded.

The fire inside became an inferno. "How could you do that?" he bellowed. "How could he do that?"

"His business consumed him. We thought it best——"

"Best for who? You? Certainly not me? This wasn't about me at all! Lance died, but you took my father away because you wanted to?" He spun away from her to find Connie standing behind her. He jerked his hand toward his wife's swollen belly. "Would you do that if I couldn't be around all the time? Deny me my child? Deny him his father?"

Connie, utterly confused and grief-stricken, reached for him, but David couldn't handle the maelstrom of emotions surging through him. He threw his arms in the air. "No! Don't." He took three steps backward, looking around wildly. He glared at his mother. "Take the taxi! Get away from me! As far away as you can get!"

He turned and stumbled away from the startled mourners, heading blindly toward the center of the cemetery. After a few steps, he broke into a jog, then a hard run, half-blinded by tears and anger. He stopped at the lake, stumbling to keep from going into the water. He turned, walking along its edge until he came to a bench and a sheltering cluster of hedges. He dropped down, burying his face in his hands.

After a bit, the fire and the tears subsided, leaving a stark numbness even more severe than it was after Lance's death. David stared at the ground, lost, unable to move. His anger at his mother, his father, still ran through him, a deep current that would take a long time to heal. At the same time, a question began to take root at the back of his mind. Who was his father? He'd asked as a child, but his mother had refused to talk about him. Did David really want to know? Maybe. Probably not. Certainly not from her.

David heard steps behind him. Thinking it was Connie, he shook his head. "I can't. Not yet."

"Oh, yes, you can," said Keli. "And you will."

David jerked to his feet. "I thought you were Connie."

"And that's one lady you owe an apology."

He closed his eyes, the pain of it all still quite raw. "I know. I just didn't need . . ."

"I heard what your mother said." Keli paused. "I'm sorry. This was not the day for that."

"Slow but steady wins the race."

David ran his hands through his hair as his muscles tensed. He fought his need to scream at the world again. Keli motioned for him to sit, and they both did, staring out at the lake.

"Keli, I don't know what I'm going to do."

The big man rolled his shoulders. "When I was about your age, my best friend, the woman I'd planned to marry, was killed in a car accident. I didn't think I'd get through the funeral, much less the next month. Or the next year. I went to see her mother one day, and I found her in the garden, plucking peas off a vine. When I asked her how she could think of peas at a time like that, she looked at me and said, 'Because the peas are still here. And it's the little details gets me through every day.'"

"You think I should pick peas?"

Keli snorted a laugh, and David felt the first easing of his pain. "Hardly. Her point was that grief can paralyze you. You can drop into its depths and never see the light of day. After Carlene's death, I didn't want to do anything because it all reminded me of her. I wanted to sit and stare at the walls, wishing her back. Not a way to live. The pain won't disappear anytime soon. It's going to hurt for a long time. There will be good days and bad, and you'll have flashbacks that'll take your feet out from under you. But if you keep your focus on what needs to be done, the things that have to be taken care of, you'll get through it."

"Slow, but steady, wins the race."

"Something like that."

David paused. "You think Lance would really want me to still go through these 'Wisdom Lunches'?"

> "He wanted you to be the leader and warrior he knew you had in you."

"I know he would."

"How?"

Keli looked up at the sky a few moments. "He left plans, just in case something happened to him. The period of mentoring he went through truly made him the man he was, helped him build the legacy you got a good look at today. He wanted you to be the leader and warrior he knew you had in you."

Silence remained a few moments, then David nodded and they stood. "OK. I'll see you in the boardroom next week." He glanced past Keli to the gravesite. "In the meantime, I need to go hug my wife and beg her forgiveness."

CHAPTER FIVE

The Wisdom Lunch Process

David entered the executive suite the next week, still aching from the events of the past few days. He and Connie had clung to each other like swimmers in deep water, and they'd spent a lot of time at the Marshall home, clustered in the den with Robert, Amanda, and Tony. They'd talked a lot about Lance, naturally, but also about what the future held for all of them.

Amanda had explained that Lance had done a lot of estate planning, so they should be financially sound. Tony's needs would be taken care of, as well as Robert's school expenses. Keli would know more about Lance's planning for the company, which was one of the questions on David's mind this morning.

He'd been in the building many times, on a Saturday, when it was empty, but the building's silence now reminded him too much of the loss they all keenly felt. It would be good for everyone to get back to the work that Lance had loved so much. The whole company had his signature on it, from the restructuring he'd done five years ago when he'd bought the company back from an investment firm to the building he'd helped design when success had meant outgrowing their previous space.

Would people ever remember him the way they did Lance? He pushed open the door on the boardroom, but couldn't bring himself to sit in any of the chairs. Instead, he stood at the window, looking out over the parking lot, until he heard Keli enter the room. David turned. "Can we do this in another room?"

Keli glanced once at the chair at the head of the table. "Of course. The smaller conference room is more suited to it anyway." He left the boardroom, and David followed, although neither of them sat down. Keli's face remained grim. "I know you don't want to do this, especially now. But it's something Lance sincerely desired for you, and I hope you'll respect that. It wouldn't be easy at anytime, and this is going to keep the grief going for awhile. But it may also help you get past it as well."

David remained silent. With the boil of pain and anger in his gut, he didn't dare. He nodded.

Keli went to an electronics armoire in one end of the room and opened the doors, revealing a computer with a forty-inch monitor. "This is how it's going to work. I know you've already set some dates with Terry. Before each meeting, you'll meet with me here. Lance had planned to do this, but he also planned an alternative, in case he wasn't around. So you're stuck with me. Lance prepared a couple of videos for you, which explains what he expects . . . expected you to learn from each meeting. I'll take you to meet with the board members, and then they'll bring you back here, and we'll debrief.

> "This is a process, a way of life, not a quick fix."

"After all five sessions are complete, you and I will continue to meet for as long as it takes or until I'm convinced you've absorbed all the principles and been able to apply them to your life. You cannot do this alone and you will not do this alone. This is a process, a way of life, not a quick fix."

David crossed his arms. "And Lance went through all this?"

"Yes. So he knew precisely how valuable this process could be in changing how you lead this company as well as the teams in it." He paused for a moment. "No man gets to be a mature leader without being a true warrior and learning from those who went before him."

"Not even you?"

Keli watched David for a moment. "You know what I do for a living?"

"You work with a baseball team."

Keli coughed. "I head up a major league franchise." When he named the team, David's eyes widened.

"So what are you doing here?"

"Because Lance was a friend. I was one of his mentors during a rough time for him, and when he bought the company back, he asked me to serve on the board. Every person on that board knew and respected Lance for what he'd accomplished. He relied on each one for guidance born out of his or her gifts. I worked with him on striving for balance in his life and how to go for a win each and every day."

> "You will need to possess a warrior like mentality to have any chance at success, and to doubt that can trip you up in the worst possible way."

Keli stepped toward him. "The idea that someone gets to the top and stays there, that he becomes a gifted leader on his own efforts and without the help of others, is a myth, a lie that can destroy you. Iron sharpens iron. We need each other, and this may be the most difficult thing you have ever had to do in your life. You will need to possess a warrior-like mentality to have any chance at success, and to doubt that can trip you up in the worst possible way."

David uncrossed his arms. "Okay. What's next?"

"Sit."

As David did, Keli booted up the computer. As the monitor lit up the room, he clicked on a series of files until he found Lance's first MP3 file. He sat across the table, and David heard him take a sharp intake of air as Lance's digital image began to speak. David winced. In the years he had known Lance, the older man had always been in good shape, working out each morning before work. Now, David could see how thin he'd been, a loss of health David had never noticed before.

Hello, David. Well, if you're watching this, it means I'm not around to guide you through the Wisdom Lunch process. I wish I were. You have so much potential, so much intelligence and drive, I know you're going to become a remarkable man and a terrific

> "It's time to get you to the next step in your journey."

leader. But you're not there yet, and I think you realize that, down deep where the bravado can't reach. We've all been there. Keli and I have especially been there. Ego and ambition, pure hard work, will get you far, but not far enough. At some point, you'll hit a wall and you won't know how to get beyond it.

You aren't quite there yet, and the goal of these lunches is to catch you before you do, before you get into the tight spots we wound up in. It's time to get you to the next step in your journey. You have a whole lot of life in front of you, and we want you to make the best of it.

Keli will be your guide. But just your guide. He cannot make you do these things, apply the principles you'll be given to your life and your work. He is one of my most trusted advisors, and a remarkable warrior, and he can be that for you as well, if you'll listen.

You are set to take over the company. You know that. But the board can and will limit your authority if they see fit. Once you go through all the lunches, you'll meet with them again, so they can see your progress see your plan for ongoing development. I, for one, have no doubt that these will get you where you need to be in order to lead this company through the next generation.

Your first meeting, as I explained earlier, is with John Holliday Jr., who is the CEO at Holliday Speedway. John Jr. is one of the most remarkable leaders you'll ever meet. He's constantly learning something new. Running a speedway is an exercise in flexibility and logistics. He has to make sure a lot of people are where they're supposed to be, often people who cannot be ordered. They have to be led. And in his business, when things go wrong, people can get killed. The races are dangerous enough, but there's no pressure in the world like having ten thousand people in the bleachers and pits with a tornado warning blasting through the air.

Lance shifted in his chair, sitting up a lot straighter, and David saw the pain in his eyes.

David, make no mistake. I am already proud of you. You are very much the third son Amanda and I never had. I see the love you have for Connie every time you're around her. This is not about correcting some wrong I see in you. It's about furthering the principles I already have tried to show you, the ones I see growing in you as a man and a leader. It is very much about guiding you toward the greatness I know you can achieve.

I know you must be hurting. That will pass. But what you'll learn now, has the potential to last forever. God bless you on that journey.

> **"It's about furthering the principles I already have tried to show you, the ones I see growing in you as a man and a leader."**

The screen went dark.

David swallowed a thick lump in his throat and turned to Keli. "OK. Let's get started."

CHAPTER SIX

The First Mark of a Mature Leader

Maintain a White-Belt Mentality

Following a curvy and wooded road, David found the Holliday Speedway nestled in a mountain cove. Keli's only instructions that morning had been to "wear boots," before handing David a map. Now he pulled into the deserted parking lot, wondering if he had gotten the time right. He was relieved when his phone buzzed with a text message from John: "Meet me in the pits."

Following the signs aimed at race competitors, David eased his Wrangler around the access road that curled around the spectators' bleachers from the parking lot to the pits and the six-lane staging area for the drag racers. It, too, was deserted except for John and two shiny, modified racers: a blue Dodge Charger and a red IROC Z Camaro. David's face tightened in confusion as he stared at all three. John waved him over, a bright smile on his face, the wind tossing his thick white hair in all directions. He had a bundle of cloth tucked under one arm.

David stopped his car, shut it off, and got out. Before he could ask, John was at his side, clapping him on one shoulder.

"I thought we'd have some fun before we started the business side of today's meeting. What d'ya say?"

Still puzzled, David shrugged. "Sure."

"Terrific!" John shoved the bundle of cloth at him. "This is a fire suit. There's a bathroom next to the concession stand." John pointed to a squat, concrete building at the end of the bleachers. "Change in there and meet me back at the cars."

"Um . . . OK." David found the open door to the men's room and went in, shaking out the fire suit, a one-piece coverall made of flame-retardant material and decorated with automotive sponsored logo patches. It wrapped tightly at his ankles and wrists, and he suddenly understood the instruction to wear boots. David felt a surge of exhilaration as he headed back to the pit area.

John's smile broadened. "You look great! Ready to race?" A dozen images from David's childhood flashed through his head as his heart thumped faster in his chest. "You bet!"

John grabbed his arm and directed him toward the Charger. "I get the red. You get blue. Now listen carefully. Follow me from the stage area around to the strip. I'll be in the right lane. You pull up into the left lane. You'll see the pre-staging beam and the starter's box, but we're going to crawl up to the stage beam, which is our starting line. That's twenty feet back from the Christmas tree."

"The pole with all the lights."

"Right. One of my assistants is running things today, and when you're ready, give me a thumb's-up, and I'll signal him. Watch the lights count down, but hold till you get the green. Then gun it for all you're worth. These babies aren't fragile. Just go, and keep it floored for the next thousand feet. At that point, you'll see the MPH lights and the finish line. Brake firmly, but don't jerk the wheel or you'll fish tail out of control. Just hold it steady and straight the entire time. You got it?"

"That's it?"

John nodded. "All you need to know for today. Just remember to brake or you'll end up in the nets. There's a helmet in your seat. Make sure it's snug. You don't need it shifting around on your head."

David found the helmet and settled in. Grabbing the wheel a moment and taking a few deep breaths. Nerves and adrenaline shot through him, and his hands shook a bit as he started the engine. Unlike the well-worn rumble of his Wrangler, the modified Charger engine roared to life, the increased torque making the entire car quiver. David let out an involuntary whoop as he dropped it into gear.

The wheel felt small in his hands, the tension on it unfamiliar and a touch frightening as he followed the red Camaro out of the staging lanes. The car responded to even a tiny shift of the wheel, and he realized how fast such a car could get out of control. They pulled onto the main track, the area behind the starting line blackened by burned rubber and heat from years of drag races.

Pulling up even with John's Camaro, David tried to calm his pounding heart as he looked down the track, which shimmered in the day's warmth, the finish line barely visible more than a thousand feet away. I can do this. I can.

He looked over at John, who watched him closely, a questioning look on his face. David took another deep breath and gave the older man a thumb's-up. John grinned and pointed at the light tree, and David stared ahead, waiting for the signal.

The yellow staging light flashed on, a bright eye high over the track. It lingered longer than David expected, then it went out, replaced in a steady countdown of lights down the pole, each one less yellow, more green. David put his foot on the accelerator, and the instant the green hit, he stomped the car into action.

The muscle car shot forward like a panther from a cage, the roar blocking out all other noise, the vibration commanding his attention. The 300-foot marker passed too soon, and the 1,000-foot marker closed in before he realized it. As the gap closed, a gleam of red to his right caught his peripheral vision. John pulled ahead, the IROC far enough ahead that David could see the decals on the rear fender.

The finish line loomed, and nothing David could do would have made a difference. He braked and the car's engine slipped back to a mild rumble as he slowed, then turned to following the triumphant Camaro down the return road and to the staging lines, where they'd first met. He didn't win, but the grin on his face and the adrenaline in his veins left him with an incredible thrill.

He got out and took off his helmet, as John emerged from his car. "That was awesome!" David yelled.

John laughed. "Did you love it?"

"You know I did!"

"Excellent! Change, and meet me on the officials' floor." He pointed at the tower on the other side of the track. "Third floor. Can't miss it."

David was still on an exhilarated high when he trotted over to the tower, trying not to whoop again, at this childhood fantasy come true. The first floor of the tower was an open area filled with cubicles, phones, and computers, but the stairs to the next floor led to a small landing with a bare wooden door. David glanced up the steps to the third floor, which ended with a steel door marked "Officials Only. No Visitors." He climbed and pushed on the door. It swung open to review a room walled by glass on all four sides, starting about four feet off the floor. Below the glass were desks filled with computers and panels of instruments he didn't recognize. A dozen or more pairs of binoculars sat around the room.

> "Experience will beat out youth every time."

John stood near the wall facing the track and motioned David over, handing him a pair of binoculars. "You did pretty well out there."

David took the binoculars, deciding John had to be the coolest old guy he'd ever met. "You still beat me."

Chuckling, John said, "Experience will beat out youth every time."

David had to grin. "So I've heard."

John's expression grew somber. "But sometimes neither help." He pointed down track. "Take a close look at the end of the track."

David raised the binoculars, focusing slowly at the area more than a quarter mile away. "The nets?"

"And the sand trap. See what's on the other side?"

David refocused. The drag race complex had been built into a long mountain cove, so that steep hills rose on all sides. Beyond the sand trap, a tall limestone wall rose more than 500 feet above the track. "You made a cut into the mountain?"

"For safety reasons. The nets and the sand trap are already above and beyond regulations, but I wanted a bit more insurance. Unfortunately, sometimes, even going the extra measure isn't enough."

David lowered the binoculars. "Someone got hurt?"

John's eyes turned dark, sad, as he stared out at the wall. "Someone got killed. The only death of this kind we've ever had at the track. One of the dragsters, the ones that require a parachute for braking. The chute failed, packed improperly. Human ignorance. The brakes failed because the pit crew didn't do the final inspection. After all, they had been inspected earlier in the day. Human arrogance."

"The race track doesn't care whether you're arrogant or simply ignorant. Both will get you killed."

He turned to David. "The race track doesn't care whether

52

you're arrogant or simply ignorant. Both will get you killed. In most businesses, you don't necessarily die, but the marketplace is the same. You can fail spectacularly if you're either arrogant or ignorant. Humility is not a weakness. It'll keep you flexible enough to be a problem-solver, and increased knowledge will keep you motivated. See that picture?" David turned. On the back of the door was a picture of a typical suburban house. Only a telephone pole stood, staunch and immovable, in the middle of the driveway."

> ## "It's what you learn after you know it all that counts."

"Wow," David muttered.

"Exactly. That's the epitome of an inflexible, incompetent worker, one who follows rules without flexibility and without the knowledge to make adjustments. I have a copy of that downstairs on the first floor as well. I keep them there to remind my team to maintain a teachable, coachable spirit in everything they do. Y'know, John Wooden once said that 'It's what you learn after you know it all that counts.' That's what makes the difference between a great leader and an average one." John put down his binoculars. "Let's go down to my office."

David followed John to the second floor, which was, again, one large open room. Windows took up the back wall, facing the track, and a broad cherry desk stood in the middle, facing the door. To the right of the desk, a small refrigerator hummed quietly near a table laden with protein bars, nuts, chips, pastries, soft drinks, and a platter of sandwiches. Beyond that, a double row of theater-style chairs faced the glass wall, looking out over the track.

The far left wall held more than a dozen certificates and awards, while a display case glistened with trophies and signed memorabilia—hats, balls, driving gloves, t-shirts. To the immediate left of the desk, however, almost within an arm's reach of the desk, a low bookcase showcased child-crafted items, candid photos of children, vacations, and an elegant woman about Holliday's age.

A light blinked on the desk phone, and John grinned. "I can tell you right now that's my youngest granddaughter. Her first dance recital is tonight. She's been burning up my cell all morning. I'll have to call her as soon as you leave."

David nodded. "Family is important."

"Amen, brother." John pushed his hair back. "I have twelve grandchildren, and they come in here on race days and count how many of their projects are on my shelves, how many times they show up in the photos." He laughed. "They started competing early for placement. But most of all, I love showing off what they've learned and achieved. I tried to instill a love of learning in their parents, and I'm grateful to see they've passed that on to their own children. We should never stop learning."

David shifted in his chair. "Lance mentioned that you wanted to discuss something like that."

John's eyebrows arched. "He did?"

After a short hesitation, David explained about the video, and Keli's changing role in the Wisdom Lunches."

The older man nodded. "Lance totally believed in the White-Belt Mentality. Looks like he even put it to use in facing his own death."

David fought a tight ache in his chest. "What is that? This White-Belt Mentality?"

Leaning back in his chair, John pointed to one of the trophies amongst the kids' display. "One of my grandson's trophies for a martial arts competition. Do you know much about the martial arts?"

"Some. I'm more of a football guy."

John grinned. "Well, the idea behind the White-Belt Mentality came from a kung fu master, one of the first, one of the greatest. He'd achieved the highest honors, several degrees of black belts. But when he died, he wanted to be buried in a white belt."

"Isn't that, like, a beginner's belt?"

"Exactly!" John leaned forward, both elbows on his desk."

> "What the master meant was that he wanted to be remembered as a teacher who never stopped learning."

A beginner is a learner. Everything is new. Everything has to be learned and applied. What the master meant was that he wanted to be remembered as a teacher who never stopped learning."

He shifted in his chair. "I've been president of this facility for more than thirty years. I started here as an official about fifty years ago. I've kept advancing, and I've stayed on top because I have a White-Belt Mentality. I stay flexible, and I'm always learning. And that's what I want to pass on to my team.

"You see, David, having a White-Belt Mentality means that you are always growing, always learning. Men can grow older, but they don't have to mature. They can keep slogging along, doing what they've always done. Living the same year over and over, never growing. But a mature leader is constantly searching to improve. They are voracious learners.

"As a mature leader, you either have a growth mindset or a fixed mindset. Fixed means you don't think you can learn anything new. But recent studies have shown that our brains demonstrate a remarkable neuroplasticity. They can continue to learn till the day we die. But in order to learn, you have to have a teachable spirit along with that growth mindset. You have to be open to hearing, to accepting and realizing that others know information, have wisdom that can help you not only as a person but as a leader."

> "As a mature leader, you either have a growth mindset or a fixed mindset."

David suddenly felt a bit wary. "Did Lance not believe I could learn new skills?"

John put up his hands. "Not at all. He'd never have let you come up through the ranks as fast as you did if he thought that." John paused and grinned. "In fact, I doubt he'd have encouraged Connie to marry you if he did."

David's brows came together. "He encouraged Connie to marry me?"

"Yep. Thought you had great potential. He didn't offer you the job just because you were dating his daughter. He offered you the job because he thought you'd be good for the company, too. And he thought the two of you would be stronger as a couple than you would be as individuals."

"So did he have in mind to help me develop this White-Belt Mentality?"

"He did! As Coach John Wooden pointed out, 'Each of us has a huge capacity to learn and to achieve. Being ever alert, makes the task of becoming all we are capable of becoming, so much easier.'"

John stood and pulled open one of the desk drawers, pulling out a leather-bound book. "As you leave today, I want to give you two tools to help you build that White-Belt Mentality. The first one is a challenge. One key to developing a growth mindset is to challenge yourself to learn one new thing every day."

"Every day?"

"Every day. This is a mental skill. 'Listen' to the learning at the end of each day. Replay your entire day in your head . . . go over how you handled things, what did you learn, what obstacles did you encounter and overcome or not overcome. Then lock it in and write it down. That's how you should end your day."

> "One key to developing a growth mindset is to challenge yourself to learn one new thing everyday."

He slid the book across the desk. "This is your second tool, we call it the MTP journal and it's about how you start each day. It's called your Morning Thought Process. When you open the journal, you'll see a place for each date. Just as you end your day with a replay, you'll start each one with a plan. It may sound 'old school,' but it works.

"At the top of each page, put the date, then you will see four categories: Important thoughts; unimportant thoughts; your prioritization of tasks; and your meetings for the day. Every day ask how you can bless someone, how you can help them grow. Unimportant thoughts need to be cast aside. Items low on your prioritization need to be delegated or delayed.

"And keep in mind that you're either growing or you're dying. If you're standing still, you're going backwards."

David took the journal and flipped through the blank pages as a knock sounded on the door. At John's answer, a young man entered and handed John a small stack of papers along with some cheese enchiladas for lunch before making his exit. John paged through them, grinning. He passed them to David.

"What's this?"

"Your stats from the race. We track everything, even a race for fun. I may have won the race, but you'll see from these that your reaction times—from the green light to braking—were faster than mine. Usually people who have faster reaction times also have faster reactions when dealing with emotions, events, and situations. This means Lance was right about you. You're gifted, but you'll have to learn to harness that. You're set to win. Just remember: 'It's what you learn after you know it all that counts and the soft stuff is the hard stuff.'"

"David, can you please pass me the 'stinkin' green chili'? Love that stuff. Thanks."

> "Keep in mind that you're either growing or you're dying. If you're standing still, you're going backwards"

* * *

Back in his Wrangler, David pulled out of the parking lot, well aware of the difference between his car and the powerful Charger he left behind – and in the remarkable difference between John's strength and experience as a leader and his own.

He tried to absorb all John had said to him, especially about how much Lance had believed in him. Lance had led him, coached him, without appearing to. That information felt suddenly like a double-edged sword, but easing the pain of Lance's loss and increasing it simultaneously.

We should have had more time!

David called Connie, who answered sweetly on the first ring. "How did it go?"

"Good."

"What did you learn?"

"That I need to keep learning. And that your father believed in us more than I realized."

Connie paused. "Us?"

"Yes. You. Me. Us as a couple. That we will be better together than we would be alone."

After a moment's silence, Connie whispered. "Be home soon?"

"As soon as I can get there. I have so much to tell you. And I can't wait for the next meeting."

"That I need to keep learning. And that your father believed in us more than I realized."

CHAPTER SEVEN

The Second Mark of a Mature Leader

Control the Controllables

The next morning, Keli met David in the company parking lot around nine. They got into Keli's car and headed out. David, still enthusiastic about the race and the meeting with John, rattled on about the details until Keli started smiling.

"What?" David asked.

"I'm just hoping you'll be as enthusiastic about all the meetings as you are this one. John said you did pretty well yesterday. He thinks you're ready to move to the next step."

David held up the leather journal. "Do you think this will help?"

"Helps me."

David paused, a little surprised. "You do this?"

"I think we all do. I know Lance did, every day. He once told me that if he skipped it, he felt 'off-kilter' the rest of the day. It helped him keep focus." Keli took a left turn. "What we've discovered is that when your day is intentional and planned, you're a more effective leader than when you stay reactive, handling business as it comes at you. A navy admiral once gave a graduation speech at a university, and he told the grads that the best thing they could do to succeed was make their bed every morning. It may sound odd, but his point was that it starts the day with an achievement, a sign that you are ready to tackle what comes next."

> "What we've discovered is that when your day is intentional and planned, you're a more effective leader."

David glanced out the window. "That actually made sense." He paused. "Speaking of a university . . ." Outside the window, the university football stadium blocked out the morning sun, slowly giving way to the practice fields and the baseball complex. "So Marla is my next meeting?"

Keli chuckled. "Good guess." He turned into a gated parking lot marked for coaches and faculty only and stopped at a guard's station. As he lowered his window, he gave the guard his and David's name, and they waited while the young man checked a list on his tablet. Nodding his approval, he handed Keli a parking pass.

As they got out of the car, Keli continued. "Actually, I'm a little jealous of you. Marla's remarkable, and I enjoy spending time with her. I learn something new every time I do. But once I take you to her office, I have a couple of meetings I have to attend. I'll be back here by the time you're done."

They entered the central building, the heart of the huge athletic complex. The lobby looked to David like one of a Wall Street corporation, with soft greens, ambers, and leather couches. But trophy cases lined the walls instead of artwork, the glittering gold, wood, and chrome awards a clear testimony of the program's successes. Memories of his own high school and college athletic endeavors flashed through David's mind, and for just a moment, a spear of jealousy toward his brother-in-law shot through him. Robert was pursuing the dream they'd both had.

David shook it off. He and Connie had talked at length about God's guidance on their lives, and both felt this was where he needed to be.

Keli led the way through a series of hallways, stopping at a double-paned glass door. The lettering on the glass read "Marla Patterson, Ph.D. Athletic Director." Keli pushed the door wide.

Inside, a bright-eyed young man stood up from behind a narrow desk. "Mr. Westering. Good to see you again."

"A.J.. This is David Jeffress. He's supposed to meet with

Marla this morning."

A.J. extended his hand and David shook it. "Of course," he said. "Dr. Patterson has asked for Mr. Jeffress to join her in a mental conditioning session she's evaluating this morning. Room 212." A.J. pointed to his right. "Just down the hall there. She's sitting in the back, and said for you just to slip in beside her. It's auditorium seating, so you shouldn't disturb anyone."

Keli nodded, checked his watch, then left as David headed in the other direction. The glass in the doors of room 212 was dark, and David paused, peering through. The room looked like a movie theater, with the back row seats at the top where the doors were, the rest sloping down to a low stage. Realizing that a video played on a screen behind the podium, he knew the class was already in session. He opened the door quietly, slipping in side. His eyes adjusted, and he saw Marla sitting in one of the seats in the back row. She motioned him over, indicating a seat next to her. He sat down as the students in front of them began laughing and nudging each other with what they saw onscreen.

Cars careened around the screen, plunging through intersections and into each other. The comic background music and the increased speed of the film turned what could have been tragic into a demolition derby of crunched fenders and furious drivers. The students laughed or winced at some of the worse collisions. David began wondering what this had to do with mental conditioning when the instructor stepped forward, stopped the video, and raised the lights.

The students moaned in disappointment, and the instructor, a short man with blond hair and muscular arms, grinned. "Yeah, I know," he said. "Funny, right? Unless you've been in one."

The students nodded and glanced at each other; clearly, some of them had been where those drivers had been. About eighteen or so young men sat in front of the room.

"So what caused all those mishaps?"

The students shifted uncomfortably, until one of them spoke up. "They ran a lot of red lights."

"And yellow," another called out.

The instructor pointed at him, nodding. "Only when they followed the traffic signals did everything go according to plan, right?"

The students called out their agreements.

"OK. Before we talk about the strength of 'going green,' let's review a few things from last week." He stepped to a podium, punched a few keys on a laptop, and a box with four quadrants on it popped up.

Marla leaned over to David and slipped him a one-sheet handout. At the top of it was the box.

The teacher continued. "Last week we talked about the four quadrants of success for an athlete. What were they?"

From around the room, students called out. "Mental!"

"Physical!"

"Social-emotional!"

"Spiritual!"

As the words rang out, they appeared on the screen, one in each of the boxes. "Remember, if we are to optimize our performance as athletes and leaders,

> "If we are to optimize our performance, we need to be working on each box or area ourselves to maximize our potential."

leading ourselves and others, we need to be working on each box or area ourselves to maximize our potential.

"So what does all of this have to do with car crashes? What was causing the crashes? Not paying attention to lights, right?" He pointed at the side of his head. "Forgetting about where they were. Maybe distracted by phone calls, texting, the radio, kids fussing in the back. Or maybe their own arrogance, thinking they could get through the intersection. So the drivers are running reds, speeding up through yellows.

"Just like in life, right. We all love to go through moments in life when things are green, and you're just rolling along. Smooth sailing. Now . . . wouldn't you want to always 'go green' when you're playing?"

There were a lot of head nods at that, including David's.

"Have you heard of 'the zone'?"

More nods as he continued. "Most of us have felt it on rare occasion, but most think it's hard or even impossible to duplicate. It's not. 'The zone' is a place that many people believe happens when you play with a free release, with no problems, with no obstacles getting inside your head. It's like everything else in life goes away, as if you've caught the perfect wave, inside the tube. Autopilot. Have you felt it?

All hands go up, and David fought the urge to shoot his into the air as well. It had been a long time, but he'd been in the zone on the playing field.

The teacher went on, prowling the stage, his charisma and enthusiasm beginning to charge up his students. "In this class, we're going to work on getting you, all of you to the zone more often, and more intentionally. It won't be something that just seems to happen once in awhile. It will be something you intentionally cultivate, with the goal of getting there every time you step on the field. We will do this through developing a series of thought processes that will help you focus on your game and your skills, and not be distracted by everything else in your life. A mental focus that will keep your head where it needs to be."

As he talked, he went to the edge of the stage and pulled three rolling white boards forward. "Traffic signals have three lights: red, yellow, green." He stopped, picked up a dry-erase marker and scrawled GREEN across the top of the first board. "The green light is your symbol for 'the zone,' for when you are playing great."

YELLOW went up on the second board. "The yellow light symbolizes when things are starting to go wrong. Your warning signs. They raise your awareness that things aren't the way they should be, that you need to be on your guard. You've all seen them, like when you throw the first pitch of a game that's perfect, the catcher doesn't even have to move his glove but the ump yells, 'Ball!'" He threw up his hands in a gesture of frustration. " So now you're thinking, great, this guy has a shoe box for a strike zone, he isn't going to give me anything, this is going to be a long day."

The class laughed and he pointed at them. "Yep. See, you've had those negative thoughts start to creep in. These build up to the red zone." He printed RED on the third board. "This is where you do not want to be. This is when things are way past yellow. We've walked three or four people and the manager is on his way out of the dugout to take us out. The team's been penalized because you've lost it, and everything is downhill from there.

"And this doesn't just happen on the field." He put down the marker and walked to the edge of the stage. "It can happen in life as well. When your gut or intuition tells you things are going wrong, and you're just not sure how to stop it." His voice dropped and he leaned a little closer to the students. "Here's a personal example from my own life. My wife and I will have a discussion, but suddenly that turns into a disagreement. I can't stop myself, my temper flares, I need to win, to be right, and the next thing you know, I'm spending the night on the couch."

As the kids laughed, he returned to the boards. "OK, back to class. I'm going to divide you into three groups. You'll circulate around the boards, one group at a time, and each group will come up with three things or thoughts for each zone. Five minutes on each board. The only other rule is that you can't duplicate what someone has already written."

As the instructor began splitting up the students, Marla points to David's handout, indicating that he should do the same. Enthused by what he's hearing, he flips the paper over and scribbles quickly as the students are writing. He's certainly had plenty of examples lately. When he looked up again, he saw that the students' lists looked a lot like his own.

GREEN

Things are going great, want to play longer
Can't wait for tomorrow to get here
I'm feeling it, no stopping me today
Things are wonderful I can do anything

YELLOW

Here we go again
Been down this road before

I'm just waiting for something bad to happen

I know what'll happen next it always does

I feel like I'm in quicksand, can't get better

RED

I'm taken out of the game

Benched

Temper out of control

Scream at my teammates and coach

David looked down at his own list:

GREEN

Things are going smooth at home and at work

Connie is happy; laughing, especially in the evenings, she feels

listened to and valued

Employees stop in because they just want to talk, maybe discuss the

future, feel needed

YELLOW

I insist on controlling the discussion

Connie goes quiet. That's when she's mad, giving up on

me she goes silent

Employees put their hand up in a conversation, trying to

keep me from interrupting

RED

I yell; lose my temper too easy

Employees stay away

No one wants to be near me, including Connie

Night on the couch

The instructor claps his hands for attention, then shows the students back to their seats. "I want you to copy all these down. First, so you'll know you're not alone. All of us go through this. Second, because you need to become aware that these kinds of negative thoughts are exactly what can trip you up. You need to recognize them for what they are and work on getting them out of your head

> "One giant step in personal growth is to recognize when things are going in the wrong direction and to learn how to stop it."

and replace them with the proper thoughts. One giant step in personal growth is to recognize when things are going in the wrong direction and to learn how to stop it. How to stop yourself and hit the reset button."

Marla tapped David's arm and motioned for him to follow her out. He hesitated a moment, looking back at the instructor, then scrambled after her. In the hallway, David couldn't hold back. "Who is that guy? He's amazing!"

Grinning, Marla led the way back to her office. "That's Wally. I hired him a couple of years ago. He's worked with everyone from the U.S.A. Olympic teams to soldiers in our country's special force's units. His specialty, is helping others become more mentally tough in competitive and combative situations. Yeah, he's one of the best sports psychologists on the planet." She paused and opened the door to her office, passing by A.J. with a nod and opening the inner door for David. The Swedish-style décor of the outer office, with its light woods and minimalist furniture styling continued into the inner office. Two walls of the rectangular room were filled with books and awards, while the two national championship trophies were centerpieces in a backlit case near her desk.

She motioned for David to sit. Her modulated alto voice resonated in the room, and her height almost matched David's. She had a thin, athletic build, and deep brown eyes. "Wally's a great teacher; we're blessed to have him. He has these mental conditioning sessions with our athletes each week, where he helps them grow and become mentally tough. Gives them the tools to help them prepare not only for the hard games but the hard spots in their lives. He's been where most of them are, so his tidbits and anecdotes really touch home with them."

"They certainly did with me. Were those all baseball players?"
"Yes, baseball. Teammates. We like to keep the teams together, especially for mental conditioning class. It helps them bond."

"Like corporate team building."
She nodded. "Something like that."
David glanced down at the paper in his hand. "I did want to ask you something about Wally's teaching on the four boxes. I thought this was a public university. How do you deal with the spiritual nature of this matrix? Isn't that like he's teaching religion?"

"Spirituality isn't always about religion. It can be very individual."

Marla shook her head. "He's not. Spirituality isn't always

about religion, and it can be very individual. But research has shown that the spiritual quadrant is the one that can drive the other three. It helps athletes—or leaders in any field—deal with those elements of life that are not totally in their control. You can usually control what you do physically, even mentally or socially. That can build in an illusion that you are in charge of all things in your life. If you don't have the spiritual preparation . . ." She paused, then went on.

"Let me put it this way. What do you do with the things you can't control? Like Lance's death? Like clients who don't get it or wrong you? What should my coaches do with inconsistent umpires and parents you can't control? How should a potential pro athlete handle an injury that changes his or her future?"

David leaned forward, shifting uncomfortably, the events of the past two weeks echoing in his mind. "I don't know. I have to admit I've struggled with that. It's not been easy."

Marla paused, then reached behind her and pulled two bottles of water from a small fridge along with a tray of assorted cheeses, meats and vegetables. She handed one bottle to David. "I know you and Lance were close. I know he was more than your boss.

More than your father-in-law. And I saw what happened at the funeral."

David held her gaze for a moment. She was sincere. Finally, he shrugged one shoulder. "It's hard. Some days are rougher than others."

"And how is Connie holding up?"

"As well as can be expected, I guess. She's pregnant. She cries when I least expect it. Now . . ."

Marla's gentle smile seemed oddly reassuring. "I have two

children and a very patient husband. Being patient with your spouse is one thing you can control."

When David grinned, she opened her bottle and continued. "One of the things we teach around here is how to control the controllables. This is how you mature as a leader. You have to not only be able to discern what you can control, but you must learn how to let go of what you cannot control. Mature leaders can control their temper; immature leaders cannot—and that goes along with an attitude that you can control everything."

"One of the things we teach around here is how to control the controllables."

Setting her bottle to one side, she reached into a desk drawer and pulled out a black rubber bracelet. "I want you to walk away today with two tools that'll help you mature as a leader and help you take that next step in your career. Even though you'll be in charge of a company, you're going to learn that there is always a next step, a new thing to learn, a new direction in which to grow."

She handed him the bracelet. Emblazoned in white were the words . . .

"Control the Controllables."

He slipped it over his hand and settled it on his wrist as she went on. "Wear this everyday as a reminder. One of things that I teach our coaches is something I had to learn myself the hard way, especially in regard to referees and umpires . . . is that I cannot control them. We give out these bracelets to remind them that they can control their temper. And they must. If they cannot control it, anger will cloud their ability to be the kind of teachers and coaches that we need at this university—let alone win games and championships and be successful. It is okay to experience emotions but it is not okay to coach or lead emotionally. We also give these to our athletes to remind them that elite performers not only control the controllables, they dominate controllables every moment of every game.

"The second thing is that sheet in your hand. Here we do just what Wally taught today, and you need to as well. It's not a fixed thing that never changes. Weekly, daily, you need to fill out a sheet like that. Ask yourself frequently: What are my yellows? What are my reds, my greens? And ask the people around you,

> "Surrender what you cannot control and dominate your controllables."

when you're green, what's the culture and the climate in your world? Talk to Connie about all this. Strive for more green, learn to recognize your yellows to reset, and surrender what you cannot control and dominate your controllables.

"If you don't you will never be the mature leader Lance believed you can be." She stood and held out her hand, which he shook gratefully. "The leader we all believe you can be and remember David, many consider these mental skills soft, or unimportant but elite leaders know these 'soft' things are the separators when it comes to building championship cultures and developing people."

David left, waiting for Keli outside the building. A stiff breeze stirred his hair, and he looked up at gathering clouds scudding across the sky. "OK, I get the control the controllables part," he muttered under his breath. "Even the red light/green light stuff. But spirituality as part of the balance . . ."

"Talking to yourself?"

David started, his face flushing, as Keli approached. "Maybe a little."

Keli grinned. "This stuff will do that. Let's go. I've got a meeting to get to and I need to get you back." He strode away and David trotted to catch up. "We can debrief a bit in the car, but we won't have long."

As they settled in and fastened their seatbelts, Keli cleared his throat. "I know this is a lot like trying to drink from a fire hose, all this information coming at you in such a short period."

> "These 'soft' things are the separators when it comes to building championship cultures and developing people."

"You're not kidding."

"But you need to get ready. It actually gets more intense from here." Keli pulled out of the parking lot.

"Seriously?"

Nodding, Keli grinned, more than a bit mischievously. "You need to meet me tomorrow morning, 5:15, at the coffee shop on Coronado Island."

David wasn't sure which bit of information in that sentence surprised him the most. "Five. In the morning."

"Yep."

"Coronado Island?"

"Right."

"Isn't...isn't that where the Naval Special Warfare Center is?"

"Correct again. And you might want to wear some workout clothes. It's going to be a whale of a ride."

CHAPTER EIGHT

The Third Mark of a Mature Leader

Possess a Sniper Focus

David still had not cleared most of the cobwebs out of his head when he met Keli at a coffee shop on Coronado Island. He'd worn his most comfortable workout clothes and running shoes. He parked and trotted up the sidewalk to the open-air deck, where Keli lounged with a bagel and coffee. David gave Keli's Hawaiian shirt and swimsuit the once-over, and Keli snorted a laugh.

"I take it you aren't going with me."

"Nope," Keli responded. "You, sir, are going to spend your morning with one of the finest leaders in the country. I'm going for a long swim. You got your bracelet?"

David held up his right hand. Marla's "Control the Controllables" circled his wrist. "And I used the MTP journal this morning."

"Excellent. Now get some coffee. You're going to need it."

David ordered a large coffee, then sat next to Keli. "Are you saying I'm going to spend my morning with the SEALs?"

Keli sat forward in the chair. "Commander Gary Fullmer will be your guide this morning. He's in charge of . . . let's just say Gary has a lot of responsibility at the Naval Special Warfare Center. He'll show you a bit about what it takes to be a SEAL, along with quite a bit of other wisdom." Keli set down his cup and focused on David. "Lance met Gary quite a few years ago, not long after Gary had become a SEAL and also an instructor here at BUD/s. They were good friends, and when Gary became the commander of basic training for BUD/s, Lance just about burst with pride."

"Is that when he came on the board?"

Keli nodded. "Lance had asked him before, but SEALs on active duty can be deployed with little or no warning. Gary didn't feel that it was fair to Lance or the rest of the board, but when he landed here, both knew the time was right." Draining his coffee, Keli stood. "Let's go. We're late."

David stared at his watch. "It's not even 5:30."

"Yep. Let's not keep the man waiting."

They walked the short distance to the main gate at the Naval Special Warfare Center, where a lean man in his late forties waited near the guard's station, his camouflage uniform blending in with the sandy beach background. Keli made the introductions, then Commander Fullmer motioned for the guard to open the gate. Keli clapped David on the shoulder, and headed back toward the coffee shop.

Inside the gate, the guard took David's driver's license in exchange for a visitor's badge, then David followed the commander toward the main building of the complex, a building constructed of concrete blocks and painted the color of sand. Over the front doors, broad letters spelling out NAVAL SPECIAL WARFARE CENTER arched over the familiar trident insignia of the SEALs. David paused, looking at it.

Commander Fullmer stopped and turned, grinning. "Don't worry. I'm not going to ask you to get wet and sandy. And call me Gary. After all, the board spends a lot of time together."

David let out a long breath. "Thanks. Actually, it just occurred to me how much respect I have for the SEALs."

"I appreciate that. Let's hope I don't do anything today to change your mind."

"I doubt that."

Gary opened the door. "We're going to cut through the building, but I thought we'd start out on the beach. The morning evolutions are underway."

"Evolutions?" David entered the building.

"You'll see." Gary led the way down a series of hallways, and David lengthened his stride to keep up. Although he was at least four inches shorter than David's six-two, Gary's wiry frame held an energetic strength. I bet he could run forever.

"Ready to Lead, Ready to Follow; Never Quit; Be Someone Special."

As they wound through the building, they passed a number of sea-blue signs with gold letters and the trident. The slogans varied, but one of the first—"Forged Through Adversity"—unexpectedly resonated with David. Before he could process that, however, they passed others—"Ready to Lead, Ready to Follow; Never Quit; Be Someone Special"—and they exited through a solid metal door and stepped out on the beach.

The sea wind whipped around David, bringing with it the frenzied shouts of men and the crashing waves of the incoming tide. In front of them, five rubber boats filled with seven men each, struggled against the ocean. As the boats rocked and bucked in the crests, the crews fought to organize and row outward. Three instructors in blue sweatshirts stood at the edge of the water, watching and occasionally calling out to the men. To David, it looked like pure chaos.

Gary crossed his arms, watching the teams closely. He raised his voice to be heard. "They're fighting the incoming tide. High tide will be about 7:30 this morning. Before then, they have to get it together as a team and get the boats out over the surf, then dump the boat, get back in the boat and then paddle them back in. And it is a race."

One of the boats almost flipped as it encountered the waves

at an improper angle, dumping three of the students into the water. Their teammates helped them back on board, but the delay cost them valuable time and momentum against the waves, as they washed back toward the beach. Yelling encouragement at each other, they struck out again.

David lost track of time as they watched until four of the five boats made it past the crashing waves. The sun was well up, warming his back, as the hardest struggling team became the fourth boat to head out, the teams bellowing their success at each other, the oars digging deep into the water.

The fifth team, however, had become completely unorganized, and one of the students dropped into the water and stalked back to the beach, screaming at his team and kicking sand as his instructor closed in on him. Oars disappeared into the water, and one by one, the men seemed to rage with frustration. All three instructors approached now, their expressions more of disappointment and resignation than anger. After a few moments, one of the instructors began speaking, although David couldn't hear the words. The boat crew turned, listened, then leapt from the boat, put their oars in the boat and in one motion, lifted the boat above their heads and trotted for the water...again. Failure is not an option.

Gary watched impassively. "This is only the first phase of training for this class. It takes time to build the teams' technical skills with the task as well as their bond to each other. After about four or five attempts, they start understanding the importance of relying on a teammate while doing their own job. We will have several of these students self-select during this phase."

David stared at him. "Self-select?"

Nodding, Gary motioned for David to walk south. As they

moved away from the boats, the noise abated somewhat. "SEAL training is voluntary. No one makes you stay here. Even the initial physical requirements to qualify are pretty stiff. In one session, you have to be able to swim five hundred yards in twelve minutes, do fifty push-ups and sit-ups each, ten

> **"Being a SEAL isn't just physical. It's mental toughness and emotional intelligence."**

pull-ups, and run 1.5 miles in less than ten minutes. All with very little rest between. So many people think that once someone's qualified, it would be easy to become a SEAL. But being a SEAL isn't just physical. It's mental toughness and emotional intelligence. You have to have a passion as well as a deep commitment. It isn't about being a strong man but a particular kind of man, a warrior. Yes, SEALs are strong, but they are also warriors who are dedicated to their service, to their country, and to each other."

They rounded the corner of one of the buildings to come on an open area of the beach that was festooned with logs, climbing walls, and ropes. A team of the SEAL students worked the obstacle course as an instructor drilled them, his deep voice echoing encouragements and demands. He walked the course with them, cajoling, badgering, teasing, congratulating. Unlike a stereotypical drill sergeant, this man struck David as being more like a coach. A very tough coach.

The result was a group of young men who persevered, even if they failed at a task the first time. They struggled, fell, got up and went at it again. David watched them, astonished at their strength, their relentless effort and commitment to finish strong. Most were in their early twenties, he guessed. "I was a football player in college," he said. "A quarterback. But I don't know if I could have done any of this."

Gary chuckled. "Attitude and mindset, David, is huge in this. If you think you can't swim five hundred yards in twelve minutes, then you probably can't. The ones who succeed in becoming SEALs may not be the best swimmers when they arrive, but they come here with the belief that not only can they swim the distance, they will. The ones who think like that, do."

> "Attitude and mindset, David, is huge in this."

As they headed back to the building, they passed a pole wrapped in white rope. Near the top of the pole, a brass bell shone in the early morning sun. Attached to the pole, a green sign indicated that this was the "Drop Area."

"What's this?"

Gary looked somber. "This is where their training ends. When a man decides to quit, that he just can't make it, he rings this bell three times and puts his helmet on the ground next to the pole. And he's done. He walks away. He's still in the Navy, but he's no longer a student in SEAL training. Come back in a week and there will be at least five more helmets lined up here."

"I would think it would be hard to quit."

"Harder as the training goes along. The closer they get to that BUD/S certificate, the more they want it."

"Buds?"

"Basic Underwater Demolition/SEAL. That's the official name of the training they're undergoing." He nodded again at the bell. "Early self-selectors tend to be men who were here for the wrong reasons or perhaps they lack the mental toughness to endure.

The prestige of being a SEAL attracts them, but for whatever reason, they can't find the inner strength that is required to be a team member. Later on, you begin to see the psychological and emotional cracks. That's when the quality of our instructors comes into play."

"The Only
Easy Day
Was
Yesterday."

As they headed into the building, another blue and gold sign near the door proclaimed, "UDT/SEAL TRAINING – "The Only Easy Day Was Yesterday." It had been placed by the class of 1989, their names and ranks listed in a box underneath.

"They never forget this place, do they?"

Gary shook his head. "And we never forget them." He led David into a conference room area, where one wall was lined with black plaques, each one featuring a photo of a SEAL, with a gold plate beneath it, listing a name and dates of service. "Our fallen brothers," Gary said quietly. "We haven't lost many, but the ones we do are honored. Each loss is felt deeply by the Teams. Our training, our bonds become a permanent, ingrained part of who we are as men and as warriors. That's one reason our instructors are so important."

David looked from the plaques to Gary, swallowing hard. "They weren't what I expected," he admitted. "I guess I was expecting drill sergeants or bullies. These guys were more like coaches."

Gary smiled a bit, and left the room, David following. "Most students need the discipline and drill of basic training, however our instructors have to dig deeper. They are the lifeblood of what we do. Without great instructors, we couldn't do what we do. You're right; they are the coaches; they set the tone and defend the standards of the work done here." He opened the door to his office and sat behind the desk.

David dropped into a chair in front of it. "I thought you set the tone."

"I may be the head, but these guys are the hands and feet." He paused. "Much like your sales reps, who are your front-line leaders. When you settle into the CEO's position, you'll

> "They are the coaches; they set the tone and defend the standards of the work done here."

set the corporate culture, but who they are and how they've been trained, will set the tone and the public face of the company. If you lead them well, oversee their training, and demand they model the culture of your organization consistently, day in day out, you have a chance for something special."

Gary leaned forward, resting his forearms on the desk. "So tell me. What do you think are the two most important ingredients of a SEAL instructor?"

David hesitated, thinking about what he'd witnessed that morning. "Knowledge. The ability to motivate a team."

"Both of those are good qualities in a leader, but there are two that are even more important to us. Humility and empathy. Humility—and I don't mean that you think less of yourself. What I mean is that you are a quiet professional who thinks of himself less often. It's remembering that this is not about YOU. Empathy is needed so that an instructor can relate to what these young men are going through. The farther you get from training, the more unlikely you are going to remember how difficult it was. An instructor has to empathize and recall his own struggles so he can connect with the student and maximize his position as an instructor.

"Lance knew this well because it's the same with sports. When he introduced me to Keli, we talked a lot about baseball. Keli told me they have to remind their coaches to have empathy because the longer it's been since they've actually played the game, the easier the game becomes to them in their mind. Our instructors have to remember how rigorous and brutal our process is."

Gary paused at a knock on his door, calling for the visitor to enter. An assistant brought in a tray with box lunches and sodas, and he set it on a conference table near Gary's desk. He saluted and exited as Gary acknowledged the salute.

"Hungry?" he asked David.

David glanced at a clock on the wall. "I didn't even realize it was lunchtime!"

Motioning for them to adjourn to the table, Gary chuckled. "Welcome to my world. Some days the training takes over everything, including your sense of time. You may not have even realized how long we stood and watched the morning evolution."

"I just kept hoping for them all to make it out, to come together as teams even if that's not realistic. I wanted them to succeed." David pulled one of the boxes closer, then cracked open a bottle of soda.

"We all do. That's part of the humility and empathy needed for the job. The process is arduous enough. It will eliminate enough students without our instructors piling more on them. We don't need to eliminate people on top of that. Instead, we

> "We have to ask ourselves, 'What's it like to be under my command?'"

need to remember to trust our process and figure out what will help each student the most, and help them find the right path. We have to ask ourselves, 'What's it like to be under my command?'"

He took a bite of sandwich and swallowed before continuing. "And we've discovered that empathetic mindset or attitude plays in all areas of life. What's it like to be married to me? What's it like to have me as your dad?

"David, Lance wanted me to pass a couple of things on to you, both of which have come out of the training here. The first is to learn what he called 'The Big Three'—the three skill sets that every instructor and leader here needs to have. And we're seeing these three things play out more and more in the corporate world and even in athletic departments at universities of all levels."

Gary leaned back in his chair and counted them off. "Number one, every leader needs to be highly relational, meaning they must be a connector, a master relationship builder. Number two, today's leader must be highly accountable where they not only hold themselves accountable, but they

> "The world has changed a lot in the last few years, and the best leaders must be relationship driven."

can hold others accountable while keeping the relationship intact. Lastly, a leader in this day and age must be highly productive. Humility and empathy will help with the first one; a sharp focus will aid in achieving the other two. The world has changed a lot in the past few years, and the best leaders must be relationship-driven. They must hold others as well as themselves accountable. We live in a world of distrust, and to earn the trust and confidence of your employees you need to be consistent and accountable to the highest standards. Only then can you hold them accountable and be able to give feedback and have them receive it without resentment. Then, together, you'll be able to build a sustainable championship organization."

"That's a pretty tall order."

Gary paused for a moment, then stood up and went to his desk. He opened the drawer and pulled something out. Returning to the table, he held out his hand. "I want you to have this."

David took it and looked at the long brass cylinder in his hand. "A bullet?"

"A .50 caliber bullet. It's a sniper's bullet."

"OK. But . . . why?"

Gary hesitated and looked away. Then he took a deep breath and continued, looking at David closely. "Lance once asked me how we trained our instructors here, how they worked to make the transition from being a Operator to training future SEALs. When I explained it, he adopted it, and this is the second thing he wanted me to pass on to you. We encourage our leaders, our instructors, to maintain a sniper focus when dealing with people."

"A sniper focus?"

"A sniper normally shoots from a far distance, using a scope that narrows his vision and focus down to everything but the target. Aim small to miss small. He has to be able to narrow his focus—while still being aware of all that is around him—in order to get the job done. And snipers may have to sit or lie in one place for hours, waiting, for the target to be achieved. As a leader, you need to see the big picture for the purposes of strategic

> "You need to be fully present. You need to be where your feet are."

development. But to be a leader with The Big Three skill set you need a laser focus on people. You need to be fully present. You need to be where your feet are."

David's eyebrows arched. "Be where your feet are?"

Gary smiled. "It's an old expression and a tool that you'll find useful not only at work but also at home. David, the concept of multi-tasking is a myth. Our brains aren't wired that way. We cannot do more than one thing at a time and give each our full attention. Think about the party host who greets you as you enter the room, all the while looking over your shoulder to see if there is anyone more important than you they need to be focused on. Or how about the teenager texting at the dinner table or you and me checking our email on our phones while our wives are trying to talk to us."

> "Mature leaders can have narrow focus and still see the big picture."

David winced. "That hits a little too close to home."

"Our brains—and our marriages—work better if we are focused on one thing at a time and don't have to shift our focus between things. If you're talking to an employee, don't answer the phone or look at your email. At home, we teach our leaders to turn off the television and give your family members your full attention. It's dismissive and disrespectful to not be fully engaged with another human being, and it sends a hidden or not-so-hidden message that you don't care, even if you do. If you can be where your feet are, especially at home, the people you lead will feel connected to you and more importantly, significant.

"David, mature leaders can have narrow focus and still see big picture. Immature leaders get caught up in the trappings of their position and can't see the forest because of the trees. Put people first.

Folks who've never been around our culture may believe that we put our missions first, since the ones they actually hear about are pretty spectacular. But we have always, always put our men first. These are highly trained individuals, who have families, and an incredible bond to each other, and many more missions to accomplish. We don't want to lose them."

Gary paused and checked the clock. "Keli will be here soon. Remember these two things: You must have a sniper focus when dealing with people. You must be where your feet are to be an exceptional leader. Second, remember to remain

> **"Elite leaders have a warrior mentality when attacking pride and arrogance."**

humble and have empathy for those you lead. Elite leaders have a warrior mentality when attacking pride and arrogance. Be a leader who is a warrior for people both at work and at home."

They finished up lunch, and Gary led David back out to the guard's station, where he exchanged his visitor's badge for his license. He walked back to the coffee shop, where Keli was on his third latte of the afternoon.

"Did you learn a lot?" the older man asked. David held up the bullet, and Keli laughed. "Yep, I've got one too."

"Seriously?"

Keli tossed his coffee cup in the trash and stood. "Lance was very passionate about being relational and accountable. That's one reason he brought me on the board. We became each other's 'Battle Buddies.'"

"Battle Buddies?"

"Accountability partners. He completely believed in the concepts of The Big Three and having a sniper focus to achieve them."

"He never mentioned any of this to me."

"It wasn't time yet. You have been on a journey since you started working at the company, and you had other things to learn first."

"So when—" David broke off as his phone buzzed in his pocket. He pulled it out to check the caller ID, stopping in his tracks as he stared at Lance's name.

Keli peered at the screen. "Ah. Must be Amanda."

Still startled, David slowly answered the call. "David Jeffress." Amanda's voice sounded hollow and filled with tears. "It's Connie, David. There's been an accident."

CHAPTER NINE

Battle in the Big House

Keli drove. David replayed Amanda's call over in his head, trying to make sense out of her garbled words. The accident, not Connie's fault. A truck had T-boned her car at an intersection, shoving her into a light pole. Unconscious. Possible brain trauma. ICU. Sixth floor. Every muscle tensed as David fought the rising panic in his gut. This can't be happening! Not after everything had happened with Lance. Was that just last week? His precious wife.

Their unborn child.

Images flashed through his mind like a movie on high speed. Connie in college, playing volleyball. Joyous times

> ## "I'll be praying for you both."

they'd shared with her family, weekend outings. The moment she'd shared the positive pregnancy test.

David hit the dash with his fist, his grief and anger raging through him.

Keli, who had been silent, spoke evenly. "I'll drop you at the front. Take the elevator to the sixth floor and turn right. The nurses' station for the unit should be right in front of you."

David glanced at him. "You've been there."

Keli didn't respond as he pulled up in front of the hospital. "I'll be praying for you both."

David glanced at him, nodded, and got out. He was breathless from tension and fear by the time he got to the ICU nurses' station. They pointed out Connie's room, one of the wide rooms with double-glass doors that circled the station. The sliding door was half closed, and he pushed it back slowly, taking in what lay before him. Connie, pale and serene, her head wrapped in bandages. A mask covered her nose and mouth, insuring a steady flow of oxygen. An IV pole next to her bed held at least four bags, all of them draining into a needle in her right arm. The left arm was held stationary in an inflatable cast, as was her left ankle. Wires emerging from her hospital gown and the bandages on her head led to a bank of machines on the far side of her bed.

"Oh, dear God," he whispered.

Amanda, who had been sitting at Connie's left, her head bowed, cradling her daughter's hand, stood up. She clutched a small Bible. Her eyes, bleary and red from weeping, still showed relief at his presence. "David!" She fell into his arms, sobbing on his shoulder. He hugged her tight, fighting his own tears. Finally, he choked out,

"Talk to me."

Amanda eased away and pulled him closer to the bed. The head of it was slightly elevated, and Connie looked as if she'd wake at any moment. David reached out and stroked her arm with one hand, the other resting gently over her swollen abdomen. "Is the baby OK?" Amanda nodded. "They think so. They have her on a fetal monitor." She gestured to one of the machines on the far side of the bed. "There's some swelling in her brain, but they haven't had to drain anything yet. They have her sedated, with the hope the swelling will go down on its own. Definitely a concussion."

Tears stung his eyes. "What happened?"

Amanda dabbed at her eyes. "The officer said her light was green, and she was turning right. This guy ran the red light and plowed into her." She took a ragged breath. "He said it could have been much worse if she had been straight in the intersection. The angle of the car saved her."

His beautiful wife. "Connie," he whispered. "Don't leave me." Behind him, the door slid open again, and a nurse and two techs entered. The nurse appraised David carefully. "Are you her husband?"

He nodded.

"I'll have some paperwork for you in a bit. Right now, we need to take her down again. The doctor wants another MRI, to check on the swelling now that she's stable."

"I'll go with you," David said, clearing his throat.

The nurse shook her head. "I'm sorry. You can't. You can wait here. We'll be back with her in a few minutes."

David tried to tamp down the surge of fear. "But I want to—"

"I'm sorry."

David crossed his arms and back into a corner of the room, next to Amanda, as they watched the process of unhooking, shifting, and wrapping tubes. Unlocking the wheels, they slowly, gently turned the bed and rolled it out of the room. The nurse looked back at them. "This will take a bit. There's a cafeteria on the second floor if you want something to eat or some coffee."

David followed them into the hall, watching as Connie's silent form disappeared around a corner. He wanted to hit something.

Amanda watched him for a few minutes. "Have you ever been with someone in the hospital?" When he shook his head, she continued. "They won't let us stay in the ICU overnight, but at least one of us can stay during the day. It'll be a long watch. I need to call Robert. Would you mind getting us some coffee?"

He stared at her. Coffee?

"Please. I don't know about you, but I'm not leaving until they kick us out. The caffeine will help."

That sounded a lot more like Amanda. The practical one. That's what Connie always called her mother. Practical. The peacemaker. Probably grown out of the years she took care of Tony, whose disabilities had required a lot of care. A lot of hospital stays. David nodded and headed down the hall toward the elevators.

His mind was a vortex of conflicting emotions. Anger. Fear. Sadness. Love. It was as if he didn't know what to do. What to say. Where to turn. Who to turn his fury on.

Just before he reached the elevator, a wooden door to his right said simply, "Chapel." He stopped, eyes locking on the word. "You." David jerked open the door and went in. The soft silence of the room caught him off guard, as did the low lighting. A backlit stained glass cross cast shades of blues, reds, and yellows over a small raise dais, where a simple podium stood. Four rows of five cushioned chairs sat empty. He stared at the cross. "Why, God? Why? I can't believe you let this happen."

> "Why God, why? I can't believe you let this happen."

David dropped down on the first chair, looking up. "Everyone tells me that 'God is love.' Really. How loving is this? What kind of God puts people through this kind of pain? And we're supposed to worship you? To shower you with love and respect . . .for what? Only more pain!"

David stood, stepping up on the platform and addressing the cross. Tears stung and blurred his eyes. He pointed his finger, his hand shaking. "How could you do this? How dare you! She just lost her father! Amanda lost her husband and now you want her daughter and grandchild, too? You let my own mother keep my father from me? And you want me to see you as my father? I don't think so! You don't deserve our love! You deserve our contempt!"

He spun, stumbled off the dais, and tripped over the chair.

With a bellow of pure rage, he kicked the chair, sending it skitter-ing down the aisle and into Keli's legs, as he stood in the door. David took one look at the older man's face and dropped to the ground, burying his face in his hands as his shoulders shook with sobs.

Keli closed the door and picked up the chair, bringing it with him as he came down the aisle. He set it in place, then sat down on the floor next to David, remaining quiet until the younger man stopped crying. "I thought that was your voice I heard yelling at God."

David took a shaky breath but remained silent.

"I've yelled at God a few times myself. Sometimes you just get so furious with Him, it has to come out." He repositioned the wayward chair. "Back in the day, my furniture wasn't so fortunate. Looks like metal holds up better than wood."

David dropped his hands, without looking up. "She could die."

"She could. But she hasn't yet. She's still here. Still worthy of prayer. And hope."

A moment of silence passed. "When the woman you loved, the one who was killed . . ."

"Carlene."

David finally looked up. "Did you yell at God then?"

"For weeks."

"Did it do any good?"

> "When we're hurting, the last thing we want is philosophy and theology"

"Made me feel a little better. Didn't change God much." Keli shifted to face David. "Believe it or not, God isn't looking to hurt us, and He hurts when we hurt."

"Then why doesn't He stop it?"

"Theologians have been asking that for years. There are a lot of answers, none of which will sound good to you right now. When we're hurting, the last thing we want is philosophy and theology. Especially from a washed-up athlete turned executive who's anything but a theologian. There are no simple answers to the why questions. "I can tell you that in time, the pain will stop being as sharp. It dulls, but there'll be a soreness, a scar, if you will. There are still times when Carlene crosses my mind, and it's been almost twenty years. Lance will always be a part of your life and his absence a hole in it. God may not choose to stop the trials in our lives, but He definitely gives us the strength and courage to deal with them.

"And Connie is still here. And in God's hands." Keli reached over and tugged on the bracelet encircling David's wrist. "This is what we've been talking about. You cannot control this, David. Connie is in God's hands and those of the doctors and nurses around here. You need to give this to God. Be here for her, pray for her, but give yourself a break."

> "Walking with God, trusting Him, and giving over to Him our uncontrollables is a process."

"Let go and let God, huh?"

Keli's smile was sad. "I wish it were that easy. Some things I have to let go of every morning because by supper I've snatched them back again. Walking with God, trusting Him, and giving over to Him our 'uncontrollables' is a process. It's a journey, a hard one. One we'll struggle with most every day. But trusting Him, walking with Him not independent of Him in the long run, will give you a peace that is beyond comprehension."

"We should pray for Connie."

"And for you." Keli put his hand firmly and caringly on David's shoulder. "You start."

The words came slowly, uncertainly, but as David asked God for help, his prayer grew in strength and confidence. He asked for forgiveness for his anger and for guidance with letting go of what he couldn't and shouldn't try to control. By the end, he had decided he would surrender and put his trust in God. When he finished, Keli squeezed his shoulder and offered up his own prayer for David and all of Lance's family.

With his "Amen," Keli looked up, watching David closer. "You good?"

David wiped his eyes. "Better."

Keli gave a low chuckle. "My friend, that is a good start. You took the first step, and that is all anyone including God is asking for." They stood up and were straightening their clothes when the door popped open, and Amanda stuck her head in. "The nurse said you were in here. You need to come quickly."

With a surge of hope spearing his heart, David trotted back toward Connie's room. He stopped, disappointed that she looked just as she had before. The doctor at her side, however, turned and greeted David. "You're the husband?"

David nodded, already suspecting he'd get that question a lot over the next few days.

The doctor checked a laptop on a stand near the bed, then looked at David again. "Right. The MRI is showing that the swelling has stopped, and may, in fact, have decreased some."

Amanda gave a small cry of joy and clutched David's arm as the doctor continued.

"We still need to watch her closely, but we're going to reduce her sedation. She'll start to feel a bit of pain, which will show on her EEG, but we'll keep that under control with different medications. If she keeps progressing, she should be awake in a day or two. With luck, she'll be coherent a day or so after that."

David walked around him and grabbed Connie's hand, resisting the urge to throw himself on her bed and shower her with hugs. "Not with luck," he muttered. "With God."

Twenty-four hours later, Connie's eyes fluttered, opening slowly. David sat by her bedside, waiting. "Take your time, honey. We have a lot to talk about."

CHAPTER TEN

The Fourth Mark of a Mature Leader

They Don't Build Dungeons

"Name?"

"David Jeffress. I'm here to see Denny Storm." He spelled his last name.

The stocky guard typed David's name into a tablet, then nodded. "You're on here." He looked up and pointed as he talked. "When the gate opens, drive straight, take the first driveway to the right. It's marked as the visitor's lot. Then check in at the main entrance. You'll be checked for contraband, then you'll be escorted to Mr. Storm. I know he left instructions for you."

David squinted at the guard. "You know Mr. Storm?" The guard nodded. "Oh, sure! He's here a lot, working with some of the cons. Prison ministry. Has made a real impact on some of them. But I already knew him 'cause my kids go to the Boys and Girls Club in the afternoon. He volunteers there, too."

David thanked him, not surprised by the comment. Keli had mentioned that Denny was "a volunteering machine." Driving on to the parking lot, he found a spot and turned off the engine. He sat for a moment, staring up at the massive gray building of the state prison, his guts in turmoil. He didn't want to do this. When Keli called and asked if David was ready to resume the Wisdom Lunches, Connie urged him to continue. More than a week after the accident, she remained in the hospital, although she had been moved to a private room. The swelling in her brain had receded, but the doctors wanted to keep her on a fetal monitor a while longer, do another MRI before dismissing her. David had tried to stay with her as much as possible, and he didn't want to leave, but both of them admitted they were beginning to get on each other's nerves. They'd laughed about it, but the tension between them had been obvious.

Amanda had relieved him today, but his reluctance to leave

Connie remained. Even now, David fought the urge to turn around and drive back. Keli's instructions to drive to the state prison to meet with Denny Storm hadn't improved David's mood. "As if I don't already feel closed in," he muttered. His conversation with Keli in the hospital chapel had helped his perspective, although the long hospital stay had left him exhausted physically and mentally. His anger at God roller-coastered; some days were better than others, as Keli had predicted.

The first drops of a rain shower sprinkled his windshield, and he sighed. "This is one of those times, however, I'd rather be on a beach with my wife."

David got out and trotted to the entrance, barely missing the heavier rain as it moved in. He shook the water out of his hair, and checked his surroundings. A small entry lobby was blocked on the far side by four guards, a body scanner, and a conveyor belt and x-ray machine for packages. He brought only a small notebook, which he sent through the x-ray machine, and dumped his change and keys in a waiting bowl. The body scanner hummed around him, adding to his sense of discomfort.

A guard waited for him on the other side, nodding a greeting. "I'll take you to Mr. Storm. He's arranged something special for you."

That doesn't sound good, David thought, as they were buzzed through a locked door. He clutched his notebook tightly as another guard joined them, and they escorted David through the visitor's room and into a long, narrow hallway. He tried to imagine what it would be like to walk this passage in shackles and he rolled his shoulders against the weight he suddenly felt.

The door at the end of the hallway led to a small anteroom

with a barred gate on the other side. They entered, and the gate slammed behind them, startling David. He became lost quickly as they navigated a series of halls and barred cells. The noise astonished him—music, catcalls, bangs, clanks, shouts, whistles, and what sounded like an out-and-out brawl. The smell was even worse, causing him to wince as they moved from one area to the other. Finally, they passed through a door that shut out all noise, leaving a silence almost as burdening as the noise. The walls were an institutional green, unbroken except for a series of windowless doors.

"What is this?"

"Solitary confinement," one of the guards responded, his tone flat as he stopped at one of the doors and unlocked it. He motioned for David to enter.

David had barely passed the threshold when the door slammed and the lock clicked into place. He jumped a bit, staring at the man in front of him.

"Welcome to solitary confinement, David."

Denny Storm sat behind a small table that held a meager spread of food he removed from a brown paper bag: two plates each held a sandwich, a small bag of chips, and a cookie. Two glasses of water sat between them. Denny stood, his close-cropped gray hair framing a ruddy face split with a wide smile. He held out his hand. "Welcome to solitary confinement, David."

David stepped forward, taking his hand. Denny's firm grip surprised David, given that he knew Denny had to be at least eighty. "Why here?" he blurted out.

The older man's eyes softened. "Uncomfortable?"

"Of course."

"Please sit." Denny motioned at the chair across from him.

"You'll find out shortly."

They sat, and Denny said a short grace before picking up his sandwich. "I'm always thankful for food, no matter how little." He took a bite. "How's Connie doing?"

David opened his chips. "Better. She's still in the hospital."

"Keli told me. You ever break a bone before?"

"In college."

"Then you can understand some of her pain over the next few weeks. The pins in her ankle are going to hurt like the devil. I broke my wrist a lot of years ago, but I still have issues with it." He twisted his watch as if reminded of the pain.

"In college?"

Denny shook his head. "The army. I'd joined right after high school, spent two years in Korea, then mustered out after ten years, took a job as a bellhop at a hotel, making nothing. I lived in a one-room studio while I worked my way up. Didn't buy a house until I was in my late thirties."

"Keli said you ran hotels."

"Providence, Inc." Denny paused for some water. "CEO by the time I was forty, after only twelve years with the company." He pointed his sandwich at David. "Not as fast as you, but I know some of what you're going through. It's dizzying. Easy to lose your way. Sometimes I felt like I was getting the bends I went up so fast."

David laughed, a sound that bounced back at him off the walls, and he looked around again. Everything in the eight-by-eight cell was the same pale color, and solid, no breaks at all. Walls, ceiling, floors, door, the narrow bed, even the toilet, one flowed into the other. Without their traces of dust and cobwebs, even the corners would have been indistinguishable. The smell reminded him of shower mold.

He gave an involuntary shudder.

"Gets to you, doesn't it?"

David nodded. "I can't believe people stay in here."

"It's why most cons will do just about anything to avoid it." He peered closer at David. "Even though as leaders, we can be really adept at putting ourselves in here."

"What?" David's eyes widened.

Denny finished his sandwich and wiped his hands. "David, people get into a pattern, a negative one, and it'll inhibit, almost kill the maximum potential that we all have, and also for those around us. It's easier than you think."

"I don't understand what you're saying."

Denny stood, pulling his chair out from the table and setting it a foot or so away. "Join me over here." David did, and Denny scooted closer, until they were almost knee-to-knee. "OK. Close your eyes. Let's do a little visualization."

David hesitated, then did so. Denny voice softened, became even, almost hypnotic. "Now. Take a deep breath. In your mind, see the walls of the cell growing even smaller, then smaller still. The ceiling is right over your head, just inches away. The only way you can be in here is to sit. You cannot stand.

"There's moisture in the air, more than even now. Cold, damp. The walls grow dark, and turn to cobblestone. You aren't deaf but you can't hear anything. The stench worsens, turns to urine and mildew, as you cannot take baths, cannot shave for months. You are alone, isolated. The only interaction is one meal at the end of the day, slid through a hole in the bottom of the door.

> "Worst of all is the realization that you put yourself in here."

You're locked in here forever, never getting out.

"Worst of all is the realization that put yourself in here. You walked through that door of your own free will." He paused. "Now open your eyes."

David couldn't wait to get them open, and he fought the urge to stand up and stretch. He straightened in the chair and crossed his arms.

> "At times, we as leaders build our own dungeons."

"What was it like?"

"Horrible," David admitted. "I can't remember feeling that isolated and alone." He scowled. "What did you mean about me putting myself in there?"

"At times, we as leaders build our own dungeons. Immature leaders do this frequently. We put up these four walls ourselves by how we think and act on a daily basis."

"How so?"

Denny stood and brought his chair back to the table, reaching for his chips. "Easier than you might think. The four walls, these are just metaphors for what we do." He took a deep breath as David joined him. "OK. Think of it this way. There are four things we think and feel that cause us to build walls. The first wall that we build is resentment. Meaning that we become resentful. Everyone has things happen in life that disappoint us. We lose people; we don't get the promotion while someone else does, etc. When that happens, it's easy for us to become resentful. Jealous. When those two emotions take hold, there is no way we can function at a high level if we start focusing on what other people have or have achieved. Resentment forces us into a victim mentality.

"Remember. Mature leaders operate with a victor mentality.

Immature leaders operate with a victim mentality. Mature leaders are overcomers. Immature leaders are overwhelmed."

Pausing for water, Denny continued. "The second wall is birthed out of self-pity, that moment when we start feeling sorry for ourselves. The worst things happen to me. I'm so persecuted. The woe-is-me attitude. I'm cursed. Nothing good ever happens to me." As Denny talked, David set aside his food, a tight, uneasy feeling gripping the pit of his stomach as he realized the man was talking about him. The words described

> "Mature leaders operate with a *victor* mentality. Immature leaders operate with a *victim* mentality."

exactly how David had felt since the Wisdom Lunches had started, resenting being pushed around, told to go here and there, who to talk to, wait on the promotion. Connie's accident, his anger with God. His emotions had all focused on how it affected him. He was totally focused on himself, as a victim.

Denny had drilled to the core of who he was . . . and he'd only gotten to the first two walls.

The older man paused. "Are you OK? You look a little green around the gills."

David's scowl deepened, but he was unsure what to say. Denny nodded, almost to himself, then continued. "Let me tell you a story. After I retired, I did a lot of volunteer work, including helping the coaches out at a local college. One fall, and for no reason in particular, the football coaches decided to make it extremely hard on the walk-ons, the kids who hadn't been recruited. I wasn't really comfortable with this bully approach to coaching, but I went along. After all, I was just a volunteer.

"So one practice they had really tough physical drills. Really put it to them. When I showed up the next day, these ten kids were huddled together, talking low. You could see they were sore . . . truly in pain. But as I looked at them, all ten of them had four letters written on their wristbands. YCBM. I looked closer. It was not only on their wristbands, it was on every inch of tape, their socks, their shoes. Everywhere. YCBM."

> "Coach, you guys can put us through the toughest drills, the hardest, but no matter what, You Can't Break Me. YCBM."

David sat a little straighter, captured by the tale. He'd been in these kids' shoes.

"So I asked them what it meant. They shook their heads, told me that I wasn't involved, just to move on. David, I didn't stand in the gap for them, do what I could when I could. They believed I went along with the other coaches. And I had. So I walked closer to them, and I apologized for the way they were treated the day before. Told them I shouldn't have remained silent. They didn't respond at first, then one kid stepped forward and said, 'Coach, you guys can put us through the toughest drills, the hardest, but no matter what, You Can't Break Me. YCBM.' I couldn't believe it, the guts and spirit these kids had."

He paused, then cleared his throat. "So, David, how much self-pity did those young men have?"

David got it. "Zero."

"Exactly. Zero self-pity. They didn't have a victim mentality. Even after all that, they had a victor mentality. They believed, passionately, that they could make the team, no matter what we threw at them. We all need to do that always, even . . . no, especially, when times are tough. No matter what this world throws at us, it can't break us. We're stronger than that. You're stronger than that. Lance believed it. So do I. You may be tempted, but you can resist taking that path."

Denny pointed at one of the walls. "That third wall is also easy to build but as dangerous as any of them. The third wall is built from impatience. We start trapping ourselves when we want things faster, easier, and want things to happen without having to wait. In this day and age, microwave food is improved, but food from the grill and stove is still better— and the slow cookers even more so. I'm sure you remember Lance teaching that things that are built to last are not built fast."

> "I'm sure you remember Lance teaching that things that are built to last are not built fast."

David nodded, smiling. "He said that a lot."

"He had to learn that the hard way, just like most of us do. There is a process to everything, but as leaders it's easy to become impatient. I'm going to tell you just as I was told a long time ago. When you're patient, it's about others; when you're impatient, it's about yourself. Mature leaders are patient; immature leaders are impatient. We have to trust the process; we have to be patient."

> "When you're patient, it's about others; when you're impatient, it's about you."

Denny stood up and went to the door, placing his palm flat on it. "This door is like that fourth wall. Some prisoners in this cell sit all day, staring at the door. It's their only sign of hope in here, hoping one day it'll open. The more time that goes by and it doesn't, their hope fades, and what settles in its place is the emotion that counselors will tell you is the most powerful of all human emotions: bitterness. That's your fourth wall, and it can be built when you don't even realizing it's happening.

> "If you want to completely destroy your ability to maximize your potential, just stay bitter."

"Now this is a very difficult emotion to deal with because it's borne out of an unjust act, an event that wasn't deserved. Anger about it dissolves into bitterness because there is no way to see retribution, what you might see as justice. But if you want to completely destroy your ability to maximize your potential, just stay bitter. Old adage: Get better or get bitter.

"If you stay bitter, you will spiral into a place of anger, resentment, self-pity, and you will never come out of it. Until we learn to forgive and move on, let go, we will never learn and grow as leaders or as people. Bitterness can stunt your personal growth more than anything else on the planet."

David crossed his arms tightly, staring at the table. He'd not taken a single note, and felt no urge to write. This guy, this old guy who seemed to have done everything, volunteering with all these clubs and organizations, seemed to be reading his very soul. Denny pushed his plate to one side and leaned his forearms on the table. "David, look at me."

Shifting uncomfortably, David looked up. Why did he want this man's approval so much? How did this guy know so much? "David, you've been through a lot the past few weeks. It's like the universe has just piled it on all at once. Not getting the promotion you'd hoped for. Lance's insistence on these Wisdom Lunches, and the way they are confronting your beliefs, forcing you to rethink things, to grow. Lance's death, and all that went on at the funeral. Connie's accident. The convergence of these events is exactly the time we feel most vulnerable, the most likely to start building these walls as a defense mechanism against the world. It's natural, but it can get out of hand. You have to guard against that, you must possess a warrior mentality."

He heard him; he did. But David couldn't shake how raw he felt. Denny was remarkable and David wanted to know him better. But not here. Not like this. He looked around at the cell, which felt even more claustrophobic than before. "So how do I prevent it? How do I get out of the dungeon?"

> "The key to getting out of this cell, of breaking down these walls, of finding freedom . . . that key is forgiveness."

Denny looked him dead in the eye and said evenly, "Son, the key to getting out of this cell, of breaking down these walls, of finding freedom . . . that key is forgiveness. Your ability to forgive and move on is essential to this process. I don't know who you need to forgive, how they've wronged you, only you know that. But there's where the key lies."

David looked down again, silent. Denny continued, more encouragement in his tone. "There are two more things you need to remember. The first is to go to hunt the good stuff, even in your failures. Find the positive people in your life. Look for that everyday win. You must hang out with the right people. The wrong people will suck the joy right out of you.

"Second, go help people. Go help

people who can do absolutely nothing for you in return. Or least who you think can't help you out. Be necessary to someone." He sat back in his chair.

"Be neccessary to someone."

"Here's an example. And this may explain to you why I volunteer in so many places. I learned about patience, about giving up self-pity from a girls' basketball team I volunteered to help, years ago, long before I retired. I was still working my way up in the corporation, and I did this for fun.

"But y'see, I used to have a stuttering problem. Every day I struggled to instruct the girls, and the harder I tried, the worse it got. Finally, one day during a pre practice talk, one of the girls put her hand on top of mine, and said, 'Coach, take your time. We don't care when we start. You have something important to say, and we'll wait for it.' From that moment, my self-pity started to disappear and my self-confidence went through the roof. My stuttering began to dissipate, and it got better every day. And I knew that I had to be for others what those girls were to me.

"Most people who live in dungeons love to help build dungeons for other people too."

"One more thing those girls taught me, that I knew I had to pass on to others. Misery loves company. Most people who live in dungeons love to help build dungeons for other people too. If they walk by someone who didn't get a promotion, they'll be the first to say 'I can't believe you didn't get that promotion. You should have. This company isn't doing right by you.' Boom, they just put up the first wall of resentment. So remember, mature leaders don't build dungeons for themselves or for

115

other people. Immature leaders live a victim mentality. Instead you need to be someone who speaks greatness into others as well as seeking the win for yourself."

Denny checked his watch. "I need to stay a while longer to finish some ministry business, but the guards will be here soon to escort you out, so I want to close by saying this. I know this is one of the harder legs of your journey, but I want to challenge you. As you leave here today, I want you to take an inventory of where you are, and where you need to be. Remember how it felt to be in this cell. Staying out of it isn't always easy. It takes work and a lot of it. But I believe that you can do it."

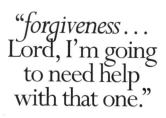

"forgiveness . . . Lord, I'm going to need help with that one."

As David followed the guards back through the maze of bars and hallways, he knew that he would never forget the overwhelming rawness of being in that cell. In his car, he finally opened his notebook and scribbled down as much as he could remember about the four walls, building dungeons for himself and for others, about all Denny had said. That the man had ended the session with his encouragement, his belief in David left an unfamiliar pride and buoyancy in his chest.

But . . . forgiveness? In his notebook, he wrote one short line in prayer: "Lord, I'm going to need help with that one."

He set the notebook aside and looked at the clouds as they scattered, letting the sun peak out again. All of a sudden, he couldn't wait to share everything with Connie, or get to the next lunch.

CHAPTER ELEVEN

The Fifth Mark of a Mature Leader

Be a P.R.O.

David stared up at the name blazoned across the top of the stadium, still not quite connecting the big man who was Lance's best friend with the name of the major league team he led. It felt a little unreal for someone that high profile to be a part of his life, much less his mentor and board member. Yet, of all the Wisdom Lunches, David actually looked forward to this one. He grabbed his notebook and headed inside.

After he checked in at the front desk, Keli's assistant led him to the executive floor, which buzzed with activity. David had not thought much about what happened within a team's off-season, assuming it was a downtime for the entire organization. But around him hummed the work of a major corporation, and his eyes widened as they approached two large, mahogany doors. The assistant pushed them opened and announced him.

Keli stood and motioned him into one of the largest offices David had ever seen. It reflected the man, he thought, matching Keli's broad, six-eight frame. Elegant but not ostentatious, the room smelled like wood oil and cigars. Cherry and mahogany woods were offset with brown leather and dark purple carpet, and windows on the far wall filled the room with light. Keli stepped from behind the desk and pointed at two sofas near two tall bookcases.

They sat, and Keli leaned forward, his forearms resting on his knees.

"First, how's Connie?"

David leaned back and crossed his legs. "Improving every day. She may go home tomorrow, depending on what the latest MRI says."

"Are things between you any better?" At David's arched eyebrows, Keli shrugged. "I've been checking with Amanda. I promised Lance I'd keep an eye out for all of you."

David paused. "You didn't mention this before."

Keli grinned. "Would you have been ready to hear it?"

Wincing, David thought of how he'd reacted at the funeral.

"Um, probably not."

"Believe me, it's temporary. I'm all about the transition at this point. But Lance knew Amanda would need a friend her own age to talk. Likewise, I think it's time for you to meet a leader your age who is where the board wants you to go. Who's already experienced a lot of these types of wisdom lunches. I know you expected to meet with me, but we've already talked a lot." He stood up. "Come on. I want you to meet Tim McGregor, my general manager and VP of leadership development, the guy who really makes this place run like a smoothly oiled machine."

They left Keli's office and headed down a wide passageway. "I'll be honest here. Tim is the glue that keeps us together. And his vision, energy, and passion for what he does here is contagious. He is the most mature young leader I've ever met in my life." He stopped and pulled open a door labeled "Press Club," making David wonder if they were going to have lunch in the press box.

Inside, however, high-end chairs and linen cloths identified the room as a restaurant. As if reading his expression, Keli continued. "We no longer need the kind of press box we used to have, so we renovated about two-thirds of the old box a while back for food and more comfort for some of our season ticket holders." He pointed out the floor-to-ceiling windows that looked out over the field. "It seats about eighty-five folks, who are willing to pay a bit more for air conditioning and a view from home plate. It's been an awesome marketing tool."

At one of the window-side tables, a young man put away his phone and stood up, a broad smile lighting his face beneath a short-cropped brown haircut. He stood a little less than David's six-one frame, but both still shorter than Keli, who clapped both younger men on the shoulder as he introduced them.

"David, Tim is a grand total of three years older than you are, but he's already walked your path. Ask him anything. Drop back by the office when you're finished."

They shook hands, then sat as a server placed burgers, fries, and sodas in front of them. They dug into the food, with Tim reaching for the 'stinkin' green chili' jar, then pausing to ask about Connie. David updated him, then after a pause, Tim's voice dropped a tone. "What about the baby?"

It was the first time in several days anyone had asked about their child. David let out a long breath. "Everyone—the docs, Amanda . . . me—we were worried for a bit, but it looks as if everything will be OK. Her regular doctors keep telling us that women are designed by God to protect their infants, and I guess she's right." Tim's eyes were bright. "That's what they told us, when Julie took a bad fall in her second trimester. But our son, Luke, is perfect. Ornery, but perfect. And we have another one on the way."

"Does it ever make you worry?"

"Ha. During her first pregnancy, I was terrified every day. Keli had just moved me into this job, and I was trying to balance the demands here—and go through the leadership training you're experiencing—with an extremely moody wife. I wouldn't trade any of it for all the riches in the world, but it was not an easy season."

"How did you get through it?"

Tim munched on a fry. "Actually, that's what Keli wants me to talk to you about, and to introduce you to how we do things here. He suggested I describe what my role is in it, and how we developed the culture here, and how that, in turn, can help you as you move forward as the CEO of your company."

> "I'd like to ask about how you built the culture here, or rebuilt it."

David opened his notebook and clicked his pen. "I'm ready."

"Good deal. But you tell me. Where would you like to start? What questions do you have?"

David paused and took a drink of his soda, his mind wheeling back through his last conversations, especially the ones with Denny Storm. "I'd like to ask about how you built the culture here, or rebuilt it. I've heard you guys have really turned it around. I'm really intrigued by what you've done. What the organization has done to put things in place that perpetuated the changes."

"Great questions! OK . . . let me back up a bit. First, I am absolutely blessed that Keli hired me at such a young age. It was entry-level at first, but like Lance did with you, Keli mentored me as I advanced until he felt it was time to move me into this position. So I already had a good grasp of the organization, what was going right—and what was going way off track.

> "89 percent of the culture of a business, a family or a team, is what people experience."

"The first thing that I did was to address the culture. We have a saying around here: that 89 percent of the culture of a business, a family or a team, is what people experience. A lot of research has backed up what we already knew to be true. And I'm not talking about signs on a wall, with motivation themes hanging all over the place. People may like those . . . or they could be skeptical of them, depending on what's going on around them. We no longer live in a world—if we ever did—where people go into their cubicles and don't interact with others. People will observe and take note of what's going on. When the people are inside the culture, what they see every day with their own eyes, what they hear, that's what counts.

"So the first thing we did was to make sure the behavior of the leaders, the managers, absolutely fell in line with whatever our messaging said. Keli wanted to emphasize consistency because he believes consistency breeds trust. Whatever we claimed or promised, that's what we did. We wanted what we said and what was experienced to all match. From the top to the bottom of the business, from the business side—ticketing, sales—to the way we develop our players and our team."

> ## "He believes consistency builds trust."

David took a break from his scribbling. "Sounds like a good plan, but how did you carry it out?"

"Glad you asked. You know that we're a baseball team."

Grinning, David nodded. "The pitching mound out there gave it away."

Tim laughed, then continued. "One of the greatest compliments one professional baseball player can give to another one is to say, 'You're a pro's pro.'"

"I've heard that."

"True. We began with the players, and we tell new signees that only men play at the major league level. With television, social media, the dollars involved, and the constant questions from the press, it takes a mature man and a mature player to handle that pressure properly. Mature men are grounded mentally, physically, socially, and spiritually. If you're not, this game will eat you up and spit you out. So if you're going to play and excel at this level you have to be a mature man—a 'pro's pro.'

"Mature men are grounded mentally, physically, socially, and spiritually."

"We broke down what that meant by using an acrostic to define the word 'pro.' Hand me your notebook."

David handed it over. Tim wrote three words down the side of a clean sheet:

Passionate
Relentless
Ownership

He returned the notebook. "Let me break those down for you the way we do for our players. You must be passionate about what you do. Passion drives everything. We spend a lot of time helping people figure out what their 'Why' is. Why are they here; why did they choose baseball; why do they want to succeed at this? We have our players spend a lot of time with the mental conditioning coaches, figuring out what their strengths are, along with their weaknesses, and their giftings. We want to find and stoke that fire, that passion.

"With the R, relentless, we want to teach them to have the attitude that they will never ever ever ever ever quit." He took a breath and pointed at the notebook. "Make sure you put a lot of 'never evers' in there. Being relentless is developing the attitude and determination that they will find a way, regardless of their circumstances, to overcome, to maintain their professionalism and their passion. A warrior mentality. Sometimes you'll hear our mental conditioning folks tell them that they have to find a way to creatively 'embrace the suck.'"

"How?"

Tim took a drink of his soda, then paused in thought a moment.

> "They have to find a way to creatively embrace the suck."

"David, this isn't always easy for us to hear, but you and I—and on both sides of us—this is a generation that has been brought up for the most part well-fed and comfortable, so to speak. We have hard times, but for the majority of us, those are temporary. We've never learned to be comfortable being uncomfortable the way earlier generations had to. We have to encourage them to persevere, to find ways to get things done. And this isn't just for the players. We have to do this as an organization as well.

> "We've never learned to be comfortable being uncomfortable the way earlier generations had to be."

"This also flows into the 'O' part of the equation. Ownership. We find that today a lot of players and employees never take ownership in what they do." The frustration showed in Tim's tense words.

"They've never been taught how! So we spend an awful lot of time and money to teach our people to take ownership and pride in what they do. It's not just about accountability—which we have to teach them as well.

"Ownership goes deeper. We have a saying that I know Keli taught Lance a long time ago: You're either coaching it or you're letting it happen. We believe that wholeheartedly in every facet of our business. Whether it's with a player, a coach, a scout or on the business end—such as in ticketing, marketing, customer relations. Everything we do needs to bring with it a sense of ownership."

> "You're either coaching it or you're letting it happen."

Tim paused to take a final bite of his burger. David stopped writing, staring at the words in front of him. He couldn't believe all the information flowing out of Tim, as if he'd been dying to share it with someone. Everything he said reflected an advanced maturity he'd not been around much. Wonder if other people will ever see me like this. And he wanted more, blurting out, "How in the world did Keli ever teach you ownership?"

Tim laughed. He pushed aside his plate and wiped his hands and mouth. "Y'know, I'll never forget the first time I experienced ownership from Keli. First, I need you to understand that almost every week, Keli and I have coffee together. It's been our routine for a lot of years. But we were running a little late one morning, and Keli decided that instead of having it in the office, we needed to walk downtown to a local coffee shop. So we walked down the street and downtown, just talking. I'm running my mouth, not paying attention, and I suddenly realize I'm alone. Keli is gone."

"Gone?"

"Yeah, like vanished."

"How do you lose a six-eight guy in an Armani suit?"

Tim burst out laughing. "I know, right? But I did. And then I did a 180, and I saw Keli about fifty feet behind me, picking up an old tissue off the ground from next to the curb. He threw it in the trash, then walked over to me and started talking, like nothing had happened.

"Now, David, I'll tell you. I felt guilty. I'd walked right by that tissue. I'd seen it, but I didn't pick it up. I didn't even think to pick it up. Not to mention that at times, I have trash in my own yard that I don't pick up, much less on the streets of the city. So Keli kept talking, and I finally couldn't take it anymore, and I asked him, 'What was that?' He didn't even know what I was talking about. I said, 'Keli. Man, you're

"Because it's my city."

the president of a major league baseball organization. What are you doing picking up trash?'"

Tim stopped and looked out at the ball diamond a moment, then back at David. "I'll never forget the answer Keli gave me that day. He looked me dead in the eye and said, 'Because it's my city.' At that moment, I knew why this man is the way he is. Not only does he take ownership of his business and his family, he takes ownership of the city in which he lives. He feels that much pride in who he is and what he's called to do. At that point, I knew the magnitude of what I was called to do. Not in the worldly sense, but in a personal sense. As long as I'm here, as long as I'm his GM, then it's my responsibility to take ownership in everything we do. And make it the best we can possibly make it."

David leaned back in his chair. "Incredible!" He checked back over his notes. "But one more question. You mentioned you started by needing to turn boys into mature men. What's your process for doing that?"

Tim glanced at his phone. "We're almost out of time, but I will tell you that this team, this organization is all about mastery." "Mastery? What do you mean?"

"Most companies strive for results. They make wins, profits, and financial growth their primary goals. And those things are important. We do have those as goals here. But if we as a team focus only on results, profits, having the best record in the league, winning the World Series, or something like that, we lose sight of our ultimate goal, which is mastery of the game, playing the best baseball, being the best team—the best men—we can be. Everything in our organization is about mastery."

"Tell me more."

"Mastery is about the best you can possibly be in every area every day. If you're good, you perform and put numbers up for a year. If you're great, you are working toward mastery, and you do it for a career. It's not about perfection. We strive for it, but we realize that may not be attainable. Just like we won't win all 162 games in a season. No team ever has. Instead, it's continuingly asking, can we master the art of playing baseball?

> "Everything in our organization is about mastery."

Can we master the art of making our people P.R.O.s? Can we master the art of turning boys into men as we sign them and they move through the system? Can we master the art of coaching and leadership, making sure each of our coaches is performing on a master level?

"And not just coaching and winning games but in developing people. We want our coaches and business leaders here to see themselves as unconditional mentors. If we're truly going to mature as a business organization, that's what our focus needs to be. We may never achieve that mastery, but it's a noble pursuit. It gets us where we need to be each and every day."

David dropped his pen, his fingers cramping trying to keep up. Feeling impressed but overwhelmed, he exclaimed, "How did you get to be so mature at such a young age?" His face flushed, but he didn't regret the question.

Laughing, Tim shook his head. "I'm not nearly as mature as you may think I am from this conversation."

"Seriously, though. I'd still like to hear how you got here. What did you read? What seminars did you go to?"

> "We want our coaches and business leaders to see themselves as unconditional mentors."

Tim sobered. "It wasn't seminars, and it wasn't just books. It was simply people pouring into my life, and me being willing to listen. And learn. We call it the Mt. Rushmore concept, and it began for me with my father and then with Keli. Everyone should have at least four people in his life who—any time, any place, anywhere—they can call those people and get truth spoken into their lives that will help make them the human they were meant to be. More importantly, to maximize their potential and be the best person they

> "Isolation is the number one killer of leaders today."

can be. Just like there are four faces on Mt. Rushmore, we want all our people to have at least four people in their life who will speak life into them—not death. Not sarcasm. Not simply results. But true honest wisdom.

"As you can guess, Keli is one of my Mt. Rushmore guys, and he's introduced me to so many people. You can't get anywhere on your own, David. Isolation is the number one killer of leaders today. Maturity has to come from growth and time with other people. You can't gain confidence without knowledge and understanding. You can't be a confident leader—and a competent leader—without knowledge and understanding. More importantly without wisdom, which is the application of that knowledge and understanding to life."

The smartphone at Tim's elbow buzzed, and he glanced at the number. "I'm sorry, but I really have to go. Please finish eating and take your time." He stood, then paused and pulled a card out of his pocket and handed to David. This is my cell number. I'd love to get back together, hang out more, especially with our families. I think Julie would like to meet Connie. There's not too many of us out there. We need to stick together."

"Gotta grow my Mt Rushmore."

David jerked to his feet and met Tim's firm grip in a handshake. "Man, I'd like nothing better than that." He watched Tim leave the room, then dropped back to his chair. He filled a couple of more pages with notes, filling in what he remembered but hadn't had time to write. Finally he paused, gazing out over the diamond again. Five lunches. So much to learn. To apply. But David felt something he couldn't ever remember feeling before. Honor. Pride. A true direction for his ambition. And a whole new boatload of information to discuss with Connie. His chest tightened as he thought about how much they'd been through since that first board meeting. How much more he loved her now—something he didn't believe possible.

This went far and beyond the two of them, however. Taking a deep breath, he wrote at the top of the next page: "Gotta grow my Mt. Rushmore."

He closed it and stood. "Next. The presentation for the board." He prayed it would be more than adequate.

CHAPTER TWELVE

The Decision

The lobby outside the company's board room looked the same. Same carpet, same artwork, same comfortable sofas, although David couldn't bear sitting right now. Unlike the room, David knew he had grown and changed considerably the last few weeks and with help, had turned his life around in some of the most unexpected ways.

When he had stood here before, he'd had his life all mapped out, certain of its path, the wrong path.

> "Lance had been right, he'd needed this."

Now he knew all too well about the uncertainties of life. At the same time, he felt stronger and more prepared for them. Lance had been right; he'd needed this. Meeting with these people had turned a spotlight on his life, ridding every aspect of shadows. His idea of leadership, his job, his future, his family . . . his wife; David now saw them all in a new light. Especially Connie, whom he loved with all his heart. Talking over these meetings with her, listening—really listening to her—had deepened their relationship in unexpected ways.

David paced slow lines in front of Terry's desk, clutching his tablet as if it were a lifeline. And maybe it was. The time had come for him to demonstrate to the board all he had learned and accepted as well as how he planned to institute these principles into his own life and the company. How well he conveyed what he was learning would mean the difference in taking over the company . . . or not.

He took three deep, slow breaths, trying to calm his nerves. He'd spent more than a week on the presentation, going over it with Connie until she told him she couldn't look at it one more time. He shared it with his mother-in-law, Amanda, who had cried and told him Lance would be proud of him.

And . . . at some deep level . . . that had been enough. Especially if he didn't get the job. He and Connie had talked over that "what if" as well, and both had reached a point of contentment. They would be fine, even after the extra expenses of the baby and Connie's absence from work. No new car—David snorted at his dreams of matching Mercedes now.

But David's life would never be the same. The way he behaved, what he thought, who he wanted to be had been irrevocably changed. It would not be easy, but there would be no going back. In more ways than he could count, he was blessed. He'd never seen that before. Now he thanked God for bringing these people into his life—

"Mr. Jeffress?"

David looked up. "Yes?"

"It's time."

He followed Terry into the main boardroom, looking at the five people in front of him, a little disappointed that Tim McGregor wasn't among them. But Keli sat at the head of the table, with John Holliday Jr., Marla Patterson, Gary Fullmer, and Denny Storm in their usual places. No one smiled, and David felt his chest tighten. Keli stood. "Are you ready?"

David nodded, and Keli walked to the end of a table, pulling back two wooden panels that revealed the AV set-up. He backed away, motioning for David to go ahead. He did, opening his tablet and plugging it into a sixty-inch monitor. As the opening slide lit up with a picture of a brown lunch bag, he turned to the board.

"First, I want to thank you all for the time you've invested in me. I know that Lance was the genius behind this series of Wisdom Lunches, but I am grateful to each of you for continuing his faith in me. I know that with him gone, it would have been easier to hire someone with more experience and wisdom. But with all that each of you has shared with me, the information, guidance, and wisdom you've passed to me, I truly believe that I can set a standard of excellence in both vision and culture that will carry this company into unparalleled success."

> "You can't give away what you don't possess yourself."

He picked up the remote and just prior to clicking on the first slide, David stopped and put down the small remote. "Before I begin with an overview and how I will be using each mark of a mature leader that you taught me as a touchstone by which future efforts will be measured in the company, I want you to know that I have made a decision. Lance always said, you can't give away what you don't possess yourself. I want you all to know that whoever is given much, much is expected and if we are to be a company that intends to be the industry standard for valuing people over results, that must start with me and I will discuss that process at the end of this presentation. Now let's begin. While experiencing the Wisdom Lunch process I ran across a quote I would like to show you from Socrates. A slide popped up with the words, "The unexamined life isn't worth living." I was living an unexamined life just going hard, keeping my head down setting goals up and knocking them down. Chasing power and money. These Wisdom Lunches forced me to examine my life and caused me a great deal of self-discovery. I realized that I needed to grow and change my thinking. I also intend to honor Lance's legacy by using the Wisdom Lunch concept to develop our leaders and legacy builders within the company. As we grow, and I believe we will, this concept will not only allow everyone in the company to mature, but it will give us the flexible yet systematic approach we need to ensure sustainable success. We must move our thinking from training people to developing or growing them. One of the key ways I plan to achieve this is through encouraging a mastery mindset in all our employees."

"What do you mean by that?" Marla asked.

"We must focus on maturing them and by helping them reach for their dreams. We will start with a number of team meetings, with the leaders first, to shift our focus from results to the process of leadership development. To focus more on people and on growing people, valuing people, developing people, a blue print process of sorts. As we encourage our employees and help them develop a focus on their own personal excellence, the results will come. Likewise, we will work with our team leaders on mastering the art of leadership by being a P.R.O., and in turn pushing that down to each person on the team. With a mastery mindset I believe that increased professionalism, relentless pursuit of individual and collective passion… ownership and accountability will be a natural byproduct out of the teams.

"Once the leaders are in place and the foundation is laid, we will be working on the culture. I've developed an acrostic that will become our company creed, if you will, to remind all employees of the marks of a mature leader and how these influence our attitudes and our goals." The slide went up behind him:

> "The unexamined life isn't worth living."

THE WISDOM CREED

White-Belt Mentality

Integrity

Sniper Focus

Don't Build Dungeons; Be Victors

Ownership

Mastery

"This creed will be given to each employee and posted throughout our campus. We want people to know what we stand for and hold us accountable. But because culture is experienced, not read on signs, each leader will be expected and encouraged to live it, to demonstrate it every day for those around them. As I've learned, 89 percent

> "89 percent of culture is what people experience while only 11 percent is what they read."

of culture is what people experience while only 11 percent is what they read."

The next slide flipped up to show the words

W.I.S.D.O.M. LUNCH PROGRAM

In one corner of the screen, The Wisdom Creed had become a small, stylized logo of a lunch bag.

"In order to encourage this conversion of a creed into a culture and to be sure people feel valued, I plan to institute a series of Wisdom Lunches for each employee. These one-hour lunches will focus on developing a life blueprint, if you will, for the employee both professionally and personally. They will be organized around what you have taught me, what I've understood from each meeting, and the takeaways for growth. Each department will have a team of lead coaches or mentors who will oversee these, and as the CEO, I, too, will be involved in the Wisdom Lunch program personally and attend as many lunches as realistically possible."

He paused and grinned at John Holliday Jr. "I am learning to prioritize." John chuckled, and David continued. "We will start with developing a White-Belt Mentality among the staff, encouraging the employees to never stop learning. In this business, which sometimes seems to change on a daily basis, a growth mindset will be key in us staying at the forefront of the industry. In addition to the Wisdom Lunch process, each employee will be given a Morning Thought Process journal and instructed how to use it. If they need to spend part of their work day researching or reading in their field, the time will be made available. If they need to take a class, attend a workshop, or finish their degree, we will find a way to help them do that."

The next slide revealed the quadrant drawing from Marla's mental conditioning handout—Mental, Physical, Emotional/Social, Spiritual. "The next step will be a bit more ambitious to implement company-wide, but we'll start with handing everyone a 'Control-lables' bracelet as a reminder. These will be green, and I plan on teaching our people the 'Go Green' traffic-light wisdom, so our people will learn how to have self awareness both at work and at home. We'll encourage the Wisdom Lunch mentors to help employees understand and differentiate their reds, yellows, and greens first, then move onto the importance of balance in each of the four quadrants of their life. My hope is that they will be as impacted as I have been by realizing the importance of all facets of their lives and the need to surrender all those things in life we cannot control.

"In addition to the Wisdom Lunches, we will be setting aside a room on each floor for prayer or mindfulness. I hope to have a mental conditioning coach on staff by the end of the year, made available to any employee who wants or needs one. I also plan to look into adding a walking track and possibly expanding our fitness room." Marla nodded her approval, and David looked briefly at Gary before continuing to address the board. "I have to admit. Meeting with Gary both intimidated and terrified me! The SEALs! Whoa!" The board member exchanged grins with David as he went on. "Everyone knows their reputation for duty and honor, the incredible physical requirements of the program and the missions they carry out. What I didn't realize, however, was the emphasis on humility and empathy they demand among their leadership as warriors. That one caught me a bit off guard; I've not exactly been the most humble man on the planet."

> "It's being where your feet are, every day, and for the leader it's about never forgetting what it's like to be my employee."

Keli cleared his throat but said nothing.

David smothered a laugh and put up a slide that said, "Maintain a Sniper Focus." "The bullet Gary gave me is in the center of my desk. While I don't feel we need to give everyone a sniper round, I do want them to see how a sniper focus can help them not only lead their teams but also maintain a humble and empathetic nature, both at work and home. Focus is not just how well you know and do your job. It's not just about driving through to success. It's also about having the ability to notice every element around you clearly as well as the big picture. It's being where your feet are, every day, and for the leader it's about never forgetting what it's like to be my employee. As a leader at home, it means that I never forget to ask the simple questions: What's it like to be married to me, to have

> "Our leaders will say more by speaking less."

me as your parent, etc.? We must lead with empathy and humility at all times.

"To try to ensure we stay on top of this, I want our leaders to have one-on-one meetings with each employee at least once a quarter, for the larger departments, and once a month for the smaller ones. We want our leaders to be Legacy Builders; we want them to understand what that means. We want our leaders to listen first and speak second. Our leaders will say more by speaking less and they will value people over productivity."

David paused, looking down a moment. "As most of you know, my meeting with Gary ended with me receiving the phone call about Connie. Keli may not have shared how badly I reacted. It was all too much following Lance's death. But it also helped bring everything that John, Marla, and Gary had tried to tell me into sharper focus. As my mother used to say, 'It was fish or cut bait time.'" He hesitated, looking at each of them in turn. "And to be honest, I almost walked away. But I knew that if I really wanted this—really wanted to mature into the man you would want to lead this company—I had to embrace it all with my heart, mind, and soul. Before Connie's accident, I wasn't sure I could. Afterwards, I knew I had to. I had to be a warrior. So I dived into the last two sessions with much more of an open mind.

"The impact of both of those sessions, with Denny and Tim,

truly changed my life. The oldest and the youngest—one is where I want to be now; the other where I want to be in the future. One woke me up; the other turned on the lights. I can't truly explain how important both of these men have come to be to me in a remarkably short time."

> "One woke me up; the other turned on the lights."

David stopped and cleared his throat before he became any more emotional, and changed the slide to a picture of a dank, dimly lit dungeon. Moss grew from the stones and mist hung in the air. "This is where I was. Asleep, imprisoned. Denny woke me up and tore down the walls. Doing the same for our employees on a company-wide basis won't be as easy. We may not be able to dive into every employee's deepest, most private feelings, but what we can do in the short term is to urge them, train them to have a victor mentality. Show them, as Denny did with me, that a victim mentality is what builds these four walls.

"We can demonstrate for them how the leaders around them are proactively avoiding these traps, and we can avoid making decisions that change their work and their lives without their

> "My goal is to also encourage and empower them to develop their own Mt Rushmores."

involvement. I believe as we grow this culture, that we can give our people the tools they need to knock down all their and our dungeon walls."

The next slide showed a close-up of Mount Rushmore. David had superimposed Keli's face over one of the presidents, making everyone laugh.

"As you've seen, much of what Tim,

140

Keli's GM, and I discussed has already been incorporated into the presentation: the changes I want to make to our corporate culture, the emphasis on each employee being a P.R.O.—one who is Passionate about life and their craft, pursues goals Relentlessly, and takes Ownership in all they do. My goal is to also encourage and empower them to develop their Mount Rushmores. Build a team of people in their lives who they can go to at anytime. Mentors who will speak the truth into their lives, bolster them when they fall, and guide them on their chosen paths.

"I believe doing this will continue to build the leaders who are already in place but also foster a legacy building program that can feed out into every aspect of our industry. We will be known not only for the best-trained employees

> **"Our employees will be our primary asset, and also our greatest strength."**

but the most mature leaders in the industry, ready to tackle anything laid before them. They—our employees—will be our primary asset, and also our greatest strength." Lance set down the remote and carefully sat on the edge of the nearby credenza. "I know with all my heart, that if I think a few meetings with you will change me forever and give me all the maturity I need…well, then I am not being honest with myself or you and I should not lead this company. If I don't possess a growth mindset and commit to a process, this is a just a hollow exercise. No, if I hope to be the man, leader and warrior I yearn to be, I must continue to meet with each of you monthly. I must have you hold me accountable and I must continue to grow personally as I apply all these principles to my life. I want you to know that I am making a life long commitment to learning and growth. I can't guarantee you or our employees that I will be the perfect leader, but I will be working on being the best person I can be, and with your help over the next months and perhaps years, we will become difference makers in the lives of thousands. I truly hope you will give me the opportunity to lead myself and the people of this company into the future."

Epilogue

One more push on the remote, and the screen went black. And David waited.

For a moment, no one moved. Marla sniffed once, and wiped the corner of one eye as she glanced at Keli.

Keli stood, applauding. Slowly, each of the other members did as well. John let out a sharp, "Whoop!" and smiles spread over all faces.

David, eyes wide, stepped backwards from the table, stunned as tear stung his eyes, too.

Keli stopped, waving his palms down, asking for calm. "OK, OK, everyone please sit. You, too, David."

David dropped into a chair as if he'd been pole-axed, still searching for breath.

Keli took a deep breath. "Well, obviously, my friend, you've made an impression. So . . . I make the motion that this board accept David Jeffress application and appoint him CEO of this organization with full power and responsibility."

"Second!"

David wasn't even sure who'd called out the second, as it sounded like at least two voices.

"All in favor?"

This time it was all five voices in unison. "Aye!"

The room erupted as Gary leapt up and yanked David to his feet, shaking his hand. "Congratulations." When Keli got to him, the big man laughed. "I guess the meeting is adjourned! Welcome aboard, David!"

David nodded, still shocked, as the other four members beamed and said their congratulations and left. Terry shut the door after the last one, and Keli sat down across from David.

"How do you feel?"

"Numb. Grateful. It's more than I'd hoped for, to tell you the truth."

"You deserve it. You've come a long way in a short time."

"But I still have a long way to go."

Keli nodded and stood. "Lance would be proud of you. Come with me."

Puzzled, David followed Keli through the side door in to the smaller, adjacent conference room. There the digital set-up for videos sat, as it had when this all began. "What's up?"

"Lance left you one more video. So I do, in fact, know how proud he'd be of you at this point. He asked me not to watch this one with you. I'm going to honor his request. You're on your own, but I'll see you first thing Monday morning in Lance's office. In your office." Keli left, leaving the room in a silence that was a complete reversal of the previous fifteen minutes. From a glorious high to this puzzled silence. David straightened his shoulders, suspecting this is what leadership was all about. He sat, and clicked play on the laptop.

Lance came up on the screen, and David paused it again. He let out a long exhalation, acknowledging how much it still hurt to see Lance alive on these videos. But he'd always be thankful for them. He pressed play.

David, welcome back. Keli has been told to play this video only if you've made it through all five wisdom lunches, have been approved by the board, and are set to take over the company. Wow! You may not realize what an amazing feat you've accomplished and journey you have embarked on, but someday you will. This just proved to me that you are, indeed, the man I knew you capable of becoming, all those years ago, when Connie first brought you to the house. She has great taste!

Seriously, you impressed me then, and I can't explain how proud I've been of you. Now that you've been through all of this and have developed your own vision for the company, I know you'll continue to grow and be a great leader and a loving husband. And you're going to be a terrific father.

Now, I want you to tackle one more thing. I firmly believe before you can settle in and be the mature leader you want to be, you need to take one more step, knock down one more of those dungeon walls, one you may not realize even exists. You need peace and restoration in your life.

Not long after you and Connie were engaged, I sought out your mother. She told me about your father, and who he was. Because they weren't married and your father couldn't be in your life on a regular basis, she truly believed that asking him to stay away was the best choice for you. She honestly had you foremost in her mind. If that was a mistake, it was made because she was a kid who didn't know any better. She made me promise I'd never tell you. I didn't agree, but I honored that request, just as your father had honored her first request.

But now I know you too well. I've been around you long enough to know that you won't have true peace until you come to terms with your father. I learned a long time ago from my high school coach, Coach Moore, that you can never be a truly mature, even a complete, man until you set aside all resentment and bitterness and find peace in the important relationships in your life.

You need to reconcile with your father before you can put the final approval on your appointment. You need to free him and free yourself. If you wish to be a whole and complete man, you need to take this step and he's in the boardroom next door right now, waiting.

You have a choice. You can walk out the front and choose not to see him, and you'll meet with Keli Monday and discuss your new role here. Or you can take the next step in your growth and open the side door and meet your father. It's up to you, and I would be proud of you either way, but I pray you will have the courage, the maturity, and the strength to take this next step.

The screen went black.

David stood up so abruptly his chair slammed into the wall. He stared at the screen, his hands clenched at his sides. How could he do this? If he knew me so well, how could he ask me to do this? A scream of rage threatened to burst out of his chest.

David walked to the window and yanked open the blinds, looking down at the parking lot. I can't do this. He turned leaning on the window sill, his eyes shifting from one set of doors to the other. He'd spent too many years resenting his absence.

His mind clicked to a stop.

"Resenting." Resentment.

No more dungeons.

Take the next step, be a warrior.

The words each of the Wisdom Lunch

> "Take the next step, be a warrior."

mentors had encouraged him to do. Never stop growing, maturing. Always be ready to take the next step.

David lowered his head and closed his eyes. Lord, you've brought me this far. If this is meant to be, please give me just what Lance said. Courage. Strength. Maturity. I realize now it's a journey. Please guide me. He looked at both doors again, this time ignoring the temptation of the ones straight ahead. He opened the side doors and stepped back into the boardroom.

He locked his eyes on his father...it was Denny Storm who stood by the windows, waiting.

David stared at him. Although his mouth opened, all words clogged in his throat.

The older man took a step forward. "Can I start with 'I'm sorry'?"

Finally, David found one word. "You?"

"I hope you can forgive me."

David moved closer. "Why?"

"Why couldn't I be around more?" David nodded. "Because, unlike you, unlike Lance, I had not learned that balance in life is more important than success. I was so determined to succeed, I lost touch with everything else. My family. My friends. Even the woman I loved."

David's eyes narrowed. "You did love her?"

"Oh, very much so. But it was the mid-80s. Greed was king, and that is no cliché. I fell right into that trap. I didn't even know she was pregnant until she was gone. By the time I tracked her down, you were nearly three years old, and she was still angry enough to throw the furniture at me. She wanted me to stay away instead of treating you both like a rest stop."

"Do you regret it?"

"Every day of my life. When Lance found out who I was, he tracked me down. He saw what I had achieved and how I'd turned my own life around, and he asked me to join the board." Denny paused. "I'm here because of you. And if you walk away—and I wouldn't blame you if you did—I will never regret agreeing to be on this board."

> "I learn every day that it's never too late to take the next step."

The two men looked at each other a moment, then David spoke softly. "I thought you were great there in that prison it was life changing for me. You really messed with my head, but I really wanted to know you better."

Do you still?"

A beat of silence passed, then David nodded. "I think I'm ready to take that next step." With a sigh, David went to his father, wrapping his arms around Denny. After their hug, Denny clapped him on the back.

"Son, I am in my eighties, and I learn every day that it's never too late to take the next step."

"Agreed, as a matter of fact, I flew Mom back in town today. I need to pick her up at the airport and ask for her forgiveness." David, pulled his car keys from his pocket. "How about all three of us grabbin' lunch today... she loves that 'Stinkin Green Chili' place, it's her favorite."

"I would love to."

As David hugged his father, he realized he'd never understood until this moment how powerful surrendering can be.

The Beginning

WISDOM LUNCH WARRIOR

The Five Marks of a Mature Leader

1. They possess a White-Belt Mentality

2. They "Control the Controllables"

3. They Maintain a Sniper Focus

4. They Don't Build Dungeons

5. They're P.R.O.s

THE WISDOM CREED

Mature Leaders Possess WISDOM:

White-Belt Mentality

Integrity (Discernment)

Sniper Focus

Don't Build Dungeons; Be Victors

Ownership

Mastery

To learn more about Rod Olson and his other products and services, including free resources and his newsletter, please visit

www.RodOlson.org

THE WISDOM LUNCH™ PROGRAM is the ultimate leadership development process and life coaching program designed to help individuals and organizations identify and pursue their dreams and goals. Coach O' Consulting works with organizations of all sizes and industries to implement the program.

For Businesses and Educational Organizations
If you would like to discuss the possibility of introducing the Wisdom Lunch ™ Program to your organization, please contact us at Coach O Consulting: www.coachoconsulting.org

For Athletic Teams, University Athletic Departments and Sport Organizations
If you would like to discuss the possibility of introducing the Wisdom Lunch ™ Program to your organization, please contact us at the Coaches of Excellence Institute: www.coachesofExcellence.com

For Individual Life Coaching and Executive Coaching
We also provide a program for individuals whose organizations do not currently offer the Wisdom Lunch ™ Program for their employees. If you are interested in participating in the program as an individual, please visit www.wisdomlunch.com or call 720-479-8100.

ACKNOWLEDGEMENTS

This book was born out of an idea that was revealed to me a few years ago to host a Wisdom Lunch ™ for my oldest son following his high school graduation and just prior to his departure for his freshman year of college. I invited 10-12 of my mentors and asked them to share two pieces of wisdom for my son that day. I wish to thank the men who attended that lunch and for the wisdom they imparted that day. It has served him well and many others have benefitted as well.

Wisdom…my colleagues and I define wisdom as simply knowledge and experience applied to life. I have been blessed to have had many great experiences in life, however the amount of wisdom that has been bestowed upon me so unselfishly by others has been humbling.

My speaking and consulting work with numerous organizations has influenced this book greatly, specifically the Pittsburgh Pirate organization and all whom I have been linked to through them over the years. The individuals that I have worked with and have become connected to have changed my life. I will be forever grateful for the unselfish leaders and coaches that have allowed me to be a part of their culture-creating and enhancing processes. I also want to thank the many leaders who did not want to be mentioned by name, but did want the principles in this book to be shared, with the hope that many leaders would be helped both professionally and personally. With too many to name, I want to thank the many colleagues I work with for their friendship, selflessness and commitment to mastery both personally and professionally. You all make me a better man, husband, father and leader, thank you.

I also want to give a special thank you to my good friend and retired Navy SEAL, who also wished not to be named. Thanks to you and to the U.S. Navy for allowing me into the SEAL culture at Coronado.

Our country is fortunate to have such warriors protecting us.

I wish to thank my son, Colt for helping me complete the story line, this book wouldn't have happened without you and I told you I would put your (last) name on the cover.

I am also forever grateful for Ramona Richards, as you help me bring my teachings to life, you are truly gifted.

To my readers, what a privilege it is to create these books for you and how humbling it is that you purchase them and share them with so many others. You will never know how grateful I am.

To all the teachers and professors of my past who can't believe that God has put a second book in me. Please utilize this book as a reminder to continue to teach the class clowns and bad kids too.

Finally, I want to thank my wife Marla for her encouragement and wisdom as both a wife and mother. You are truly the greatest gift God has ever given me, you are my crown jewel. And to my children, Colt, Connie and Lance I am forever grateful for your hearts and willingness to put up with "Coach O".

I wish to thank God for His word and the principles in this book. All wisdom comes from the Father and through His son, Jesus Christ who lived them out. The insights and any good in this book comes from Him, and whatever may be wrong in this book is on me...as it should be.

ABOUT THE AUTHOR

Rod Olson or "Coach O"

Tabbed as the Coaches Coach, he is an author, inspirational speaker, facilitator and consultant. Rod has trained thousands of leaders nationwide in the worlds of sport, education and business. After a 20 year College coaching career, Rod founded the Coaches of Excellence Institute, a 501c3 nonprofit organization along with the Coach O Consulting Group. Rod speaks and inspires leaders across the globe where his clients range from Fortune 50 companies to the US Navy SEALS Instructors. Currently, Rod helps direct the Coaches development for the Pittsburg Pirate organization among others. Rod is also the author of the highly acclaimed short novel (and prequel to *The Wisdom Lunch*) on coaching and leadership, "*The Legacy Builder: 5 Non-Negotiable Leadership Secrets*" in bookstores everywhere. Rod resides with his wife and family near the beautiful mountains of Denver, Colorado. For more info or to book Rod for your next event, go to: www.RodOlson.org and get a daily tip from him on Twitter @CoachOTip

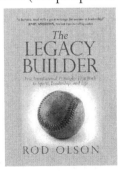